Cursed Talent

3rd

of

The Caeteran Tales

by

Susan Stradiotto

This is a work of fiction. All the characters and events portrayed in this novella are either fictitious or are used fictitiously.

Edited by Amy Bishop
Book cover and interior design by Susan Stradiotto.

Printed in the United States of America

First Printing, 2019

Print ISBN-13: 978-1-949357-06-6
eBook ISBN-13: 978-1-949357-07-3

www.susanstradiotto.com

Praise for The Caeteran Tales

★★★★★

"If you enjoy reading about women on top of their game with a twist of science fiction, you'll love this read."

~ Mira Kanehl—The Sorceress' Child Series ~

★★★★★

"Elle and Javine are so vibrant and lifelike, and the whole novel just buzzes with their chemistry and tension. I would recommend this to fantasy lovers and non-fantasy lovers alike."

~ Goodreads Reviewer ~

"I love the author's linguistics which enrich the Caeteran experience, a Tolkienesque Flare!"

~ Amazon Reviewer ~

Table of Contents

Waking Hours 7
Breakfast 11
Dion'Mor 23
Mountain Pass 27
Kav-Astahr Tienne 41
Many Meetings 51
Alphiné's Duty 57
Kurkuma Extract 59
Cavali Cengal 73
The Meeting, Part 1 83
The Meeting, Part 2 93
Flaming Plains 99
Flare 107
Fire Dance 115
Journey Home 127
Phillary House 131
Dressmaker 135
Evaluation Iméra 147

Entrants Gather 155

Testing Begins 163

Chemical Flare 173

The Interlude 187

Psychological 191

Cera and Gregor 201

The Aftermath 203

Conference 211

Evaluation Complete 223

Armagnac 229

Appendices

Character List i

Glossary v

Acknowledgements ix

About the Author x

Waking Hours

Elle sur Phillary
Phillary House
Terrináe, Caetera
16 de Lares, c3683

A WEEK SPENT IN a strange land and induced to stay only the night before, Elle had fallen into bed exhausted both mentally and physically. She was certain that she would have slept just fine with no regard for her surroundings. But when Sirena, the plump little Keeper of Phillary House, had offered some tea for relaxation, Elle didn't refuse. Who knew how much Yster had been influencing her sleep since her arrival? If she would be sore after whatever awaited tomorrow, as Gregor had promised, she likely needed the rest. The tea did help her sleep for a while. But since waking, hours of darkness had hung outside and within her small room. She flipped the covers plaintively and rose from the bed, padding to the window and considering her situation.

Keepers, Benefactors, Mentors, what other positions are there? Elle wondered.

The lack of artificial light frustrated her in these early sleepless hours. Had she been able to read, she might have rifled through Gregor's office to see what else she could learn about this place and her Benefactor. As it was, the moons had ducked to the far side of the sky, the Clarets no longer glowed, and the only light was from the smattering of stars and a faint white glow shifting against the backdrop of the otherwise black night sky. Elle had seen images of the Northern Lights back on Earth, but they were usually green and bright; these were less prominent and were only clear due to the absence of city lights.

She could have gone for a run, but again, the dark...and to where? Surely not knowing the area, she'd be lost in no time. Then there was the matter of safety. *Stranger in a Strange Land,* she thought. How ironic that seemed, and she wondered if Heinlein had known about Terrináe when he'd written the book. Boredom it was—until others stirred.

Elle reflected on Induction. So many people on the edges of their seats. All so normal, yet so...*not.*

She reflected on the days before. All so peaceful, yet so...*not.*

The courtyard beneath her second story window remained silent this early as she stirred around her regret for Caleb, but she felt surprisingly little remorse over having so easily decided she wouldn't return to Earth or to him. He was successful and attractive. He probably already had a line of girls from work who couldn't wait to *comfort* him.

Then there had been the strange, ghostly voice that had echoed to her as she'd entered the carriage. What the hell had it meant by the "dark and flaming path?" And being knocked out to *go home*? Beyond the kidnapping, something else—she couldn't say exactly what—was simply wrong about this situation.

The glowing in the sky faded as a thin, lighter blue outline formed over Ovest Idris, signaling the arrival of dawn. The stable doors below swung outward into the yard. Niccolai—or Nicco, he'd said—stepped through, pushing the doors to their widest point. Two cavali, tall and silvery-white, loped into the yard. He disappeared into the stable, returning with saddles, blankets, and bags and laid them out on the decking near the awning.

Nicco whistled and a silvery caval approached the platform to be saddled. Elle turned from the daybreak scene to dress. Time to see what was on the agenda for the day.

Breakfast

Gregor Phillary
Phillary House
Terrináe, Caetera
16 de Lares, c3683

GREGOR PHILLARY PUSHED THE pteryx eggs around his plate, his throat too tight to swallow. Sirena, his Keeper, cleaned around him and put bread in the oven to complete the morning meal. When she'd arrived in the kitchen, she'd scolded him for being awake so early and quickly scrambled the eggs. Food was her typical way of caring for the House and its Benefactor. He barely noticed her scuttle. The events of late and his impulse decision to take on a ward with an apparent psychological Flare had put him in a state of turmoil, and as his subconscious tried to make sense of his rash actions, his dreams had been haunted. He'd left his bed, dressed, and come to the kitchen in an effort to clear his mind, but the images hadn't yet dissipated.

Cera sur Gustava played a featured role in his dream state. No longer a member of Gustava House, she had become the new Votara d'Alphiné, priestess of the Second Holy Unity, upon her recent return to Terrináe from the Éhrosi Isles. Her predecessor, Victoria had passed—a death of age alone—the cycle prior, leaving the position vacant for a long period. Given that Entrant Season in Terrináe had been coming to a close, he'd expected the vacated priestess's position to be filled. Entrants who'd chosen to stay over the prior six Induction periods would begin school, and the voteri played a large role in their education. Until he'd seen Cera wearing the rose-golden robes in the wings at the Odeum during Induction, he hadn't known of her return.

The dream left him with the bone-chilling cold of the cavern temples, dank aromas, and dimly lit passageways as well as the anguish and guilt he'd borne at the time. The stones had been rough under his boots and palms as he'd climbed the cliff's face to the Second Cavern Temple—penance he'd believed. The priestess, Victoria d'Alphiné had welcomed him into the sanctuary of the Second Holy Unity. She'd maintained her poise while already showing signs of age. Gregor shifted in his chair at the breakfast table and rubbed his neck where she'd cradled his head into her shoulder and offered comfort for his turmoil. If only the simple embrace had been enough to absolve him of the sins he'd committed against his love. Cera.

This morning, he tried to pretend all was well as his Keeper, Sirena, bustled around the kitchen. With the bread in the oven, she smiled left the room, and Gregor dropped his head into both hands, allowing the dream to live again.

> *As Victoria d'Alphiné showed him into a bedroom carved into the tunnels, it had been dark, lit only by banked embers on a small hearth. On the bed, Cera crouched in a corner wearing a plain, dark robe. Cera sur Gustava—still a member of Gustava House, Gregor believed—was wispy and frail. She'd lost enough weight that her eyes were sunken and hollow, and she recoiled further into her corner as she caught sight of Gregor.*
>
> *"Benefactor Phillary?" Cera said weakly, distantly, coldly. The formality stung. Even sequestered, she'd learned*

of his appointment. "Why have you come?" she asked.

He turned from her, fighting his thick throat and burning eyes. He projected: 'I needed for us to heal...together.'

"Don't!" Her command carried an edge sharper than a blade's.

He turned to her in shock, but she'd changed from the childlike fetal form to something feral, poised on the balls of her bare, dirt covered feet. Every fiber in her body held the angry pose as if coiled for the strike.

No formality remained, nor was there tenderness or frailty in her voice. "Do. Not. Speak to me through your mind." Then quieter, she added, "It reopens the wounds," and turned to the wall.

"I'm sorry," said Gregor. "'Tis hard to speak the words necessary."

Cera's lank hair swung as her head snapped back to Gregor. "And how do you think it is to hear them? To hear the same voice that eased me through the pain of his knife whisper again in my mind...to hear the same voice that loved me once so tenderly turn sharp and partner with that bastard's Flare to convince me that I enjoyed being mutilated...to feel that betrayal brush against my mind in the most intimate of ways, now? How easy do you think that?"

Gregor pushed the plate away and stood, crossing the kitchen to the side window. Her words bit then and now. Those words and his actions would haunt him for as long as he drew breath. In the yard to the side of the house, Ashe and Misty had their own breakfast, then the view blurred as he returned to that day 242 cycles before.

"Cera, I cannot forgive myself for the wrongs I have done," said Gregor, moving to the edge of her bed.

She flew from her position and from his side. She watched him wearily, then turned away, hugging herself around the waist—below where her lovely breasts once protruded. Quieter then, she said, "As some reason still lives in a remote place in my mind, I know it was him. I know he controlled you...controlled me...controlled us." She swallowed, the thinness of her neck exaggerating the action, "I know you broke through and saved us both."

Gregor watched the embers outline her profile with an orange glow. Streams of her tears shimmered in the dim light, and he wanted to hug away her pain. For once, he'd wished his psychological Flare to be stronger so that he could relieve her of the burden with touch as could the vile vasiliás, but as events had proven, that was a dangerous Flare. It had been selfish of him to have come. While he'd believed facing the situation was best, she clearly had not. He rubbed sweat from his palms on his thighs, stood, and reached for her, but again she scurried away.

"Cera, please. We were so close before. Can't we work on healing together."

She said nothing, glared at him, and before she turned to the hearth, she crumbled before him once again, her lip quivering. The moment she had given up before was mirrored in her eyes—the time when Gregor had stood over her, empty of his own consciousness, and forced through Renauld's will to view her as an object rather than the cherished lover she'd been.

"Cera?" he asked, "Please...forgive me?" His words trailed as hope ebbed.

In Phillary House kitchen, Gregor closed his eyes, inhaled, and held his breath. As he exhaled little by little, Cera's tormented words wouldn't stop until they'd run the full course. They pulled him back into the vision heart-first almost against his will, most definitely against reason.

"Gregor," she breathed, but still wouldn't look at him. "When Renauld tortured me, that was one thing." She sniffled. "When he made me watch, bound and gagged, as he tortured you, I thought that was the worst he could do." Wiping furiously at her tears, she continued, "But when he made you connect with me mentally and encourage me to bear my fear as well as the physical pain as he sliced through

my breasts in slow, deliberate strokes, my soul broke."

She hugged her thin frame tighter, then added, "All I see and what I associate with that darkest moment are your empty eyes. I do not have it within myself to forgive you for the sins I know weren't your own. That is my sin, and I must bear it alone."

He gulped, losing certainty with every word she spoke that their bond could overcome the darkness. His own tears ran freely into his beard. He turned toward the door and projected back to her: 'I am so very sorry, love.' He hoped she'd remember those as his last words in her mind.

'Gregor?' Her honey sweet thought reached his mind, a warmth that he'd once known well. At least her mental voice wasn't angry as she projected his

name. He waited for whatever she would say as a final farewell.

"I will be going to the Éhrosi Isles on the morrow. Given my psychological Flare, I have been accepted as an Éhrosa. Though that will be hard with my deformity, I will try. Votara d'Alphiné has also offered me sanctuary in the Second Holy Unity's Temple d'Éhrosi." There was a long pause, then she projected: 'My life is given to the loving service of Alphinus and Alphiné. I pray that you find peace, and I regret that I am unable to help you in your search.'

Gregor left.

Gregor blinked several times in succession, shaking off the vision. Mental communication leaves a mark unique to the possessor of the thoughts and his or her talent to project. Gregor could count on a single hand those he'd known with a psychological Flare strong enough for telepathy, and each had his or her own voice. Renauld's had been comforting like a blanket on a cool night, and he'd used it in terrible ways. Gregor had always compared Cera's to honey; it was sweet and made his mouth water. He hadn't consumed the warm golden sweet since that day in the Second Unity's temple, but he'd tasted it when he'd awoken that morning and now as her final words echoed through his memory.

He shook his hands out at his sides then strolled to his office to grab a book that would be a necessary reference. Preparing for the journey would surely offer a better distraction than eggs. With book in hand, he turned to the front door and his caval, Ashe.

Before exiting, a thud sounded from upstairs—a long-unused door closing. *Elle,* he thought, pausing in his tracks. He harbored uncertainty about selecting her during Induction, though somewhere inside, he knew it was in her best interest. Best how remained to be seen, and that he'd finally chosen an entrant for Phillary House would cause quite the stir around Terrinae. At least his actions would give the appearance that he was performing his Benefactor duty, even if that was not his intent. What a surprise her Flare had been—the only thing that could have convinced him to choose an entrant. Even untrained, she'd projected with clear words and imagery. *Her* mental voice was the trill of a bird high in a tree singing to the skies.

Gregor dipped his head. Knowing that Sirena would prepare Elle to join him and Niccolai for the journey, he refocused on preparing for the day's trek to the vineyard, pushed open the door, and stepped into the morning.

Dion'Mor

Dion'Mor Ailig
Tienne h'Ìosal, Caetera
16 de Lares, c.3683

OUTSIDE AILIG'S TENT, THE Suebhi stahm broke camp. The second night of the journey from the far reaches of Tienne h'Ìosal, the Flaming Plains, had passed without event. The convoy transported a small herd of caval and would arrive at Gregor Phillary's vineyard with enough light to rebuild the tents. The cavali were for trade with the Terrinian, but Ailig had also received a message from Gregor that he needed to meet on the behalf of Terrináe's royalty. Ailig had worried over that for days as the small people from the city in the Idris Mountains didn't normally take interest in the stahmen of the plains.

"Aithar?" his daughter's voice drew him from his worry.

"Màiri. Mo khinde. Come," Ailig held out his arms for his daughter, and she fell inside as if they were the safest place on Caetera.

Màiri was the spitting image of her father, but with a woman's curves. She was near his height, though slighter, and bore the same golden coloring in hair and skin. Excluding the amber eyes, she was unlike her deeply bronzed older sister whose mother had been J'thungi.

They took a seat on Ailig's blankets, the ones the stahm had yet to roll and store for the last leg of the trip. Màiri fidgeted her hands in her lap.

"Mo khinde, speak of any subject. You are future Dia'Mor, and we must speak our concerns openly," Ailig encouraged.

"It is so. I ask you once more to reconsider giving Haize to the gneàrps—"

"Do not use that word, mo khinde." His words were strong, but patient. "We must lead by example. If we wish our people to work with the small ones, we must do the same."

"Yes, Aithair." Màiri hung her head, warmth crawling into her cheeks. She was learning the ways of her father's nobility, but she slipped into calling them by the old term for rodents far too often.

Ailig placed a long finger on her chin and lifted her amber eyes to his own. “We have discussed this. You know the sacrifice I make to build trust with Gregor.”

“But she is different, Aithair,” Màiri pleaded on behalf of the caval. “Cengal is stronger in her.”

“It is true that I work to find the weakest spirits to offer in trade, but it is not always possible. Gregor is able to form cengal with the beasts.”

She snapped her head up at that. “They are not beasts!”

Ailig gave her a look that said all of a father’s words of warning without a sound. When she bowed her head, he continued, “He has sworn to care for their spirits as well as their physical needs. Trust must be established. Gregor is worthy of trust.”

His eyes lit in anticipation as he asked, “Shall we ride, mo khinde?”

MÀIRI RELENTED TO AILIG'S admonishment but didn't agree. As far as she was concerned, no word spoken would convince her that Haize should be traded outside of the Suebhian stahm. Her opinion mattered little, as her aithar was Dion'Mor. Ailig had given her everything she'd ever needed, had coached her in the ways the Mors so she could assume his mantle one day, and his regard for the small man was sound. Gregor had proven himself over time, so she would defer despite how much it pained her. She respected authority and wisdom, but she secretly suspected that her cengal abilities with the cavali were stronger than her father's. She swallowed and nodded, then asked with a smile, "Have I ever rejected riding, Aithar?"

Mountain Pass

Elle sur Phillary
Nord Idris Mountain, Caetera
16 de Lares, c.3683

GREGOR HAD PREDICTED ELLE'S body would hurt by day's end accurately the prior evening. The aches and pains would assuredly be more than she had ever known. She uncomfortably shared a saddle with a silent rock, also known as Nicco, who rode behind her. Her knowledge was limited, but the saddle seemed large for a single person. Still, with two, space was limited. It wasn't her idea of traveling in comfort. Her back agreed, viewing the experience as more akin to torture, especially given that Gregor had said it would be dark before they reached their destination.

Elle looked up through the broad leaves at the purplish sky. She'd hoped to gain some idea of how many hours were left in the day, but all she was able to glean was that their sun was about midway through the day's—iméra's, if she was to use the local term—journey. There were likely many hours before darkness fell. She slumped.

Gregor rode ahead of Nicco and Elle, out of their sight. That left Elle alone with the infuriating man who refused conversation. Having already replayed the prior week in her mind and coming to no further conclusions, she tried to pass time taking in the surroundings. There were no signs of a city or civilization. Not being the outdoorsy type, she was at the mercy of these two men for any type of survival.

Her fingers unconsciously fidgeted with the heavy, coarse fabric sitting in front of her. It served as a ladder and rode slung over the caval Misty's neck as they traveled. Even at six and a half feet, Gregor and Nicco still required a ladder to swing into the saddle. Elle looked down past Nicco's arm. She'd never been afraid of heights before. In fact, she'd relished thoughts of moving up. She'd equated it with status. But here, falling would hurt, maybe even land her with a broken bone or two. She needed a distraction.

"What do you enjoy doing in your free time?" Elle tried again to strike up a discussion with her sour riding-mate, hoping for more than the single-syllabic answers she'd gotten so far.

“Hunt.” Nicco didn’t move with the response any more than the usual rocking from the oversized horse’s gait.

“What do you hunt?” She pressed for more.

“Boar.”

“There are boars here?”

“Yes.”

Elle concluded that the conversation was pointless. “Do you have any compound words in your vocabulary?” she asked tartly.

“Yes.”

She threw a hand in the air as best she could in the cramped position. “I give up.” She shouldn’t, but a one-sided discussion without direction seemed futile.

The rocking motion should have been lulling, but discomfort in Elle’s lower back stabbed with every tilt of the beast’s long step. In their constant forward motion, through the woods, Elle descended into a trance where the white-wooded trunks took on a life of their own, circled and passed endlessly on either side. Leaves and sticks crunched below Misty’s hooves, and her nasal exhalations broke the woodsy silence at regular intervals.

Even though Gregor had assured her safety, she wasn't sure what was supposed to make her trust that. Maybe she should search for...what? A weapon? A way out? Escape? On a mountain? In an entirely different dimension? What an illogical and hopeless situation. There wasn't another answer that she could see, so she went along. And waited.

When Misty carried Nicco and Elle into a small clearing, Gregor returned to meet them, riding Ashe. "'Tis a wonderous day, and we make good time. Ianarius blesses our travels. We stop here to rest and refresh the cavali," he called before he dismounted in a single leap from the saddle.

Elle gasped, certain that landing would result in a twisted ankle, broken leg, or worse—blood. He landed gracefully and stood. Her rush of adrenaline ebbed, and she put away the worries.

"Oh, thank God!" she said, overly grateful for the imminent relief from the saddle.

Nicco reached around her, dropped the fabric ladder, and held her hand as she found her footing on the rungs. She concentrated on the descent, but a strange vibration ran down her arm from where he steadied her. Elle looked up, past their joined hands, and into his sharp aqua eyes. Did they warm? Did he warm? A bit?

A muscle worked in Nicco's jaw. He broke eye contact and released her hand.

Elle fell, landing hard on her backside. "OW!" Her curiosity toward him transformed to scorn as he stifled a snigger. "Why did you let go?" she snapped.

No answer. Nicco swung his far leg over and dismounted in a smooth motion landing in a crouch at Elle's side.

She stood, dusted the decaying leaves from her backside, and walked gingerly to relieve the strain in her back and hips.

"Niccolai, grab the books," Gregor commanded as he freed Ashe to wander the clearing. The man had two modes—authoritative and eloquent. Elle couldn't tell which one to expect from moment to moment.

Nicco fished in the saddlebags and pulled out two hard-bound books. He handed one to Elle.

Looking at the spine, she read aloud, *"Suebhian: The Language and Culture of the Flaming Plains?"* Elle looked to Gregor who stood bent in half with his fingertips dangling just above his boots.

Standing, he pointed and said, "You will start with that."

"What do you mean. 'I will start with this?' We've been riding for hours. I have no clue where we're going. I have no clue why we are traveling. And *now* you want me to sit down and read?"

'Maybe you could give me a bit to recover?' she thought indignantly.

Gregor shot her a sly smile. "Not read. Learn the language. You will recall...I said there are expectations." He paused as his words sank in. With his eyebrows raised, exercising that authoritative side, he added, "And I never told you to sit."

"Fine." Elle's whole body tensed, and she fought a childlike urge to stomp a foot. "How do you say, *'Where can I pee?'* in—" She looked at the book spine. "—Suebhian?"

He held out his arms, indicating the entire forest around the clearing. Elle pushed through some brush, hoping there were no poisonous plants, and took care of business. Dripping dry was one of the least joyous things she could remember. Groaning, she pulled up the entrant-grey pants and stepped over the log and brush.

She returned to the clearing with her lips still pressed tight at the fact that Gregor's command had been so strong with simple words and a mere look. She'd prided herself on being at the top of her game in her corporate life, but his demands were a stark reminder that she'd passed through some wormhole and didn't know the rules of Caetera, the norms, or even what dangers she might face.

Striving for the strength she'd known before, she asked, "What if I refuse to learn the language?" Movement and deep-throated laughter to her side grabbed her attention.

Nicco leaned up against a wide white tree trunk, obviously amused at her effort. "I will help her, Gregor."

"Oh, now you pipe up?" Elle snapped back at her riding *non*-companion.

Gregor gave Nicco a single nod, then locked eyes with Elle, "You won't refuse for long. You'll find it, shall we say...useful." He turned away, patted Ashe, and disappeared into the woods.

With scrutiny on the only other person in the clearing, she bit again at Nicco, "Since you're so ready to help, why don't you start by telling me what Suebhian is. And what are the Flaming Plains?"

He flipped his hair from his eyes and sat. "Bring the book."

Elle rolled her eyes, "Do you plan to answer my question?"

He didn't look at her but nodded. "The Flaming Plains are grasslands farther ovest than the mountain face where Gregor's vineyards lie. Suebhian is the language spoken by the tribespeople of the plains."

"I don't want to sit. I've been sitting in the saddle all morning," said Elle. Their pace was frustratingly slow compared to her city life, and she questioned why she needed to learn the language. Not to mention when she'd need to be proficient. Elle also wanted to know what had happened to Sonia and Braeden, and the other entrants. "Why are we going to the vineyard today? I thought we were about to start school."

"You have two and a half mádi before school begins. We will be back long before that." He answered.

'Vague and partial answers must be in the water,' the sarcastic part of Elle said, then added, *'or the Kool-Aid.'* The fact that he was offering more than one-word answers kept her questions rolling, "Are you in school?"

"Requittance." The answers shortened.

"I'm sorry, requittance?"

"Yes, the period after schooling where you remain in the Benefactory House."

Elle crossed her arms and chewed the inside of her lip. She'd have a raw spot there by the end of the day. "The vineyard..." she revisited her question, "why are we going?"

"To pick up your caval."

His words were matter-of-fact, purely normal, but they turned Elle's saliva to dust.

'Fabulous,' she thought. *'I've never even ridden a normal horse. How the hell do they expect me to ride one of those giants?'*

His eyes darted up to Elle's, looking almost accusing. She didn't understand the nasty look; she hadn't responded, had given him no reason for anger or accusation. "Is there more?" she prodded.

Nicco shook his head, brow furrowing as if he searched for an answer. "There is a meeting with one of the tribes," he said at last.

"Oh." Now Elle understood why the language would be useful. Of course, there was no way she could hope to become fluent before they arrived at nightfall, but maybe she could learn a few key words. "I guess we should get started in that case." She paced slowly in front of where Nicco rested against the white trunk.

Nicco opened the book and started with the customary introduction. He promised that once she got the hang of the guttural r characteristic to the Suebhian language, she would fly through learning the rest. Elle didn't believe for a minute that she could coax her tongue and throat into making those coughing and hacking sounds. But she *had* overcome all coursework challenges set before her to date. Having started, by her force of will, she was doomed to mastery—whatever it took.

"Ar vaschen d'ehrlichen," Nicco said with ease.

Elle's repetition didn't resemble the sounds. She tried again with little success as she walked. She tried using her hands, turning them at the wrist and spreading her fingers to encourage the words to form correctly. She tried positioning her body in different ways. At length, she stopped, facing her instructor with shoulders slumped.

"Ar," he paused, touching either side of his throat with a thumb and forefinger. "You feel it here, in the back of your throat. Arrrrrr..." he finished, emphasizing the gurgle.

"Arrrrrr...matey," Elle said with a small smile.

Nicco's eyes were blank. Either he failed to understand or didn't think it funny. "Not quite, but closer."

Elle widened her eyes and said, "Okay then..." She refocused her efforts. The attempt to imitate him down to the throat touch was also no help.

Finally, he stood, grabbed her hand, and placed it on his own throat so that she could feel the rasping and humming that made the necessary sound. Her hand tingled and she looked up at him questioningly as she *felt* his frustration. She placed her other hand on her own throat, something clicked into place, and she repeated, "Arrrrrr..." It was at least close.

Nicco nodded his approval and almost smiled, but just as quickly pulled back and averted his eyes. In doing so, he emphasized each syllable of the full words of greeting, "Ar-va-schen-d'ehr-lich-en."

Elle repeated. It resembled the Suebhian greeting.

She smiled proudly.

He nodded again. "For short, you can say, *ar vaschen.* It doesn't shorten it *much*, and it is a very informal way to greet someone, but it does save you some of those harsh sounds."

Gregor emerged from the woods and signaled it was time to leave. Elle's hips groaned in disapproval as she climbed the ladder, and her back screamed its protest as she sat into Misty's saddle. Nicco, lithe and unfazed by the long hours astride, slipped in behind her. When they were both settled, he loosened the reins and nudged Misty into a canter, following Ashe and Gregor.

For some time, Elle practiced the words of greeting with Nicco, but soon they fell back into the tense silence that colored the morning's ride. After countless hours, dark blanketed the land, and the floral incandescence began to light their downward path from the crest of the mountain that now stood between Elle and Terrináe. The long-legged cavali had an evolved grace in navigating the steep, rocky terrain. With Misty's steady gait, Elle struggled against the sleep that threatened to nestle her into Nicco's unintended embrace.

NICCO SCANNED THE DARKENING forest. He wished she would just go to sleep so he could relax for a moment. He rubbed his jaw. He'd ground his teeth all day, clenching to prevent himself from responding to Elle's telepathic thoughts. Gregor's words from the prior night, *'If you*

heard her, you are not to let her know,' looped in his mind continuously and had also grown tiring.

Of course he could hold a conversation, if it weren't for the brain's gymnastics, trying to adhere to his Thrice Bound Oath, and fighting off an unwieldy arousal. Elle's accursed fresh scent, like that of the blue-eyed vernas floating in the baths' waters, hadn't helped his cause in the slightest. He'd tried all day to envision something gross or painful, anything undesirable, but hangnails and broken bones failed to squelch his yearning.

He cursed his addiction and, in present company, hated himself for how he'd used so many women. As Elle sank heavier in his arms, sleep claiming her, he thanked the Unities for the brief reprieve. It wouldn't be long before they would come to the edge and they could give legs to the cavali. Fuck if he didn't need the jolt that came with the cavali's flight, fueled by the magic of the plains.

Kav-Astahr Tienne

Elle sur Phillary
Border of Tienne h'Ìosal, Caetera
16 de Lares, c.3683

THEY HAD LEFT BEHIND the glow of the Noctilucent Clarets by the time the white-wooded forest ended in a line and the grassland began. Misty trotted up alongside Ashe and nuzzled her dual, nubby horns beneath the other caval's chin. Elle was certain that the knobs would feel like heaven digging into the muscles in her lower back. She sighed.

Gregor sat astride Ashe, leaning forward, scrutinizing something the distance. Elle followed his gaze through the dark expanse of grass to the speck of light. In the distance, the bonfire seemed like a lone candle flame hovering in the darkness.

"It appears that the tribe arrived early," Gregor said, not glancing from the flicker.

"Yes. Are you ready?" Nicco replied, his voice anxious and vibrating with anticipation.

Gregor turned. Despite the dark, his eyes sparked. "I am. Shall we?"

Elle felt, more than saw, Nicco's nod. Gregor leaned over and pet Ashe's neck, then Misty's. He looked intently at Elle with a quirked brow. "Hold on."

Nicco moved both reins to one hand, and his other arm snaked around Elle's waist. Before she could protest, a glimmer of white in her periphery launched into motion, and their own mount lurched forward. The first few strides jarred her aching body, but Nicco pulled her tight and moved them together counter to Misty's run. It lessened the impact. Elle gasped, trying to breathe. Then the ride smoothed into a glide, wind whipped through her hair, and Nicco loosened his grip. Misty kept to Ashe's tail, who carried Gregor toward the quick-growing fire.

Elle's breath returned, but in spite of the now easy ride, awe had stolen her words. She dropped her head back and was unable to resist the smile pulling at the corners of her lips. She could have been in a car, a convertible under the stars. Of all the stories about journeys along Route 66 in the

American Southwest, this is how she'd imagined it would feel with the top down, speeding along at night. The high permeated every fiber of her being.

"How fast do they travel?" Elle screamed over the wind noise.

"Dunno."

Elle started, "How—"

"Kav-astahr tienne. Magic," Nicco cut in.

Elle didn't understand, but she let it drop. Talking in the wind was too much, and she wanted to enjoy the simple pleasure—wherever it came from.

As they neared the fire, new features of the landscape grew, and shadows deepened—a house, stables, an outbuilding, and fields of what Elle assumed were vines. Flames towered over the heads of shadowy onlookers moving around the bonfire.

Nicco's arm encircled her waist once again, and Elle tensed as Misty's gait downshifted.

"Relax. Ride with her," Nicco said softly in her ear. She did the opposite. The hot breath at her ear reminded her Caleb. "Trust me, it'll be easier," Nicco added.

It was more words than the man had spoken for the second half of the day. Remembering the start of Misty's gusting ride, Elle drove thoughts of Caleb away and tried hard to comply. Several bounces in the saddle and they were back to the rocking canter within a hundred yards of the roaring fire. Shadowed faces turned to meet the new arrivals.

"Ahem..." Elle said, "You can let go of my waist now. I think I can stay on at this speed."

Silent and slow, his strength released her, and he returned both hands to the reins. Misty stopped beside her fellow caval and Nicco dropped the ladder, holding Elle's hand as she dismounted. The same twinge ran up her arm, and Elle wondered about Nicco's special power. It didn't have the same calming effect as Yster's mentor's touch, but something was there when their skin touched.

Elle was better prepared this time and didn't think she'd fall if he let go, but he eased her all the way down before releasing her hand. In a repeat performance of their earlier break, he dropped to a crouch at Elle's side, but this time, he didn't rise, looking past her.

When Elle turned toward the fire, Gregor had dismounted and was in a similar crouch, but with one knee and one hand placed onto the ground. His eyes focused on his hand rather than the three men who approached where he crouched. Nicco grabbed Elle's hand. The vibration crawled up her arm again as he jerked her to his level. As soon as she was down, he jerked his hand away, cracked his neck, and emitted a small moan.

"What's going on?" Elle whispered as quietly as possible.

Nicco put a finger to his lips and mouthed, "Wait."

Elle figured he was probably right. They weren't far enough away from the aboriginal-looking men approaching their benefactor to have a conversation about the matter. She looked around to see where they might escape. *'Why did we approach the natives anyway?'*

"Shh," Nicco said and pointed to Gregor.

Confused, Elle started, "I didn't–"

"Shh," he hissed again.

Elle bit down, teeth clenching and holding her questions inside.

The man in the center, the tallest of the three, stood in front of Gregor with arms crossed over an immense bare chest. His words were in the guttural tongue Elle had only recently learned. Gregor responded without looking up from the ground, but the most Elle understood was the *Ar* that he vocalized and assumed it to be the formal greeting.

The men's faces were still in shadow with the light from the distant fire flickering at their backs. The two on the sides held staves taller than they stood. Center-man had long hair on the crown of his head tied into a ponytail that swung as he looked from one companion to another and conferred in lowered tones.

Gregor waited.

After trading some banter, center-man held out a hand. Gregor bent his forehead to the ground before he accepted the arm. Then he rose, hands locked on the other's forearm, and they bro-hugged.

Elle's eyes darted a question to Nicco. Apparently, the gesture was natural to the male species no matter where, when, or what world.

Nicco shrugged.

Gregor motioned in their direction and brought over the trio for introductions. "Ailig, this is Elle."

With a closer view, all three men had the same blond hair, with two braids running the length of their crowns from front to back and wrapped around the high ponytails to secure them in place. The sides and back of their heads gleamed bald—not trimmed. There were rows of markings along their jaws and the sides of their scalps that Elle couldn't make out in the dim and distant light of the fire.

She crouched frozen as the behemoth at the center of the three reached out an arm. Uncertainly, Elle stood. Nicco did not.

This man, Ailig, was a head taller than Gregor, yet Elle only reached Gregor's shoulder herself. Holy shit, she felt like a child in front of them. She'd never seen someone so large. Basketball players back home had nothing on this group. And after the formal greeting Gregor offered, Elle hadn't a clue what Ailig expected of her. She searched Gregor's face for an answer.

Reading her correctly, Gregor coaxed gently, "A simple handshake is fine for tonight."

The sheer size of Ailig's hand threatened to swallow her arm. Elle reached forward—slowly—and placed her hand in his waiting palm. She drew her brows together, tilting her head. There wasn't a mentor's calming. Nor was there the hum she felt with Nicco's contact. But she felt immediate deference to this man, which probably had to do with his sheer size. He squeezed her hand lightly and raised it to his lips.

He brushed a soft kiss over her knuckles, holding Elle's eyes. Something about his facial features was strange, a longer than normal forehead maybe. In the silvery light and shadows cast by the two moons, Elle couldn't see enough of him to read an expression. Ailig glanced at Gregor and released her hand, standing to his full height.

Elle tried his language, "Ar vaschen d'ehrlichen." It was slow and broken and it sounded like she was coming down with the flu. Thank goodness the cover of darkness hid her blush.

Ailig beamed and through his throaty accent, replied in English, "On behalf of honesty." Then to Gregor, he made some more foreign hacking noises.

One of the guardsmen offered Nicco a hand. With permission, he rose at long last from his crouch.

"First time on a caval for the day," Gregor said on the lilt of a laugh. Then he looked toward the house and addressed Nicco, "She won't make it long."

That comment and meaningful look toward the house pushed Elle into motion. "Hold your horses!"

The three tall men flinched, and Elle held up her hand in surrender to attempt to ease the apparent insult. She continued, "First, I'm standing right here. Secondly, you're not sending me away already."

The two men on either side of Ailig stepped in front of their leader and brought their staves across their bodies, at the ready. Elle flinched away as Gregor and Nicco both held hands up as if to surrender.

Five sets of wide eyes focused on Elle, all with eyebrows raised. She looked beyond the men between herself and the fire. Where there had been motion around the fire as they'd approached, all shadow figures were now still, watching and waiting for whatever would come next.

Gregor spouted off some quick and harsh-sounding Suebhian. Ailig placed a hand on each of his guards, and both returned to his side, at ease.

"Elle." Ailig took a step closer, looming, and said, "*Hairse—*" he spat the strongly accented *horse*, "—is bad word to my blood. Yer bed 'tis the better choice fer now."

Elle's breath hitched again—the size of this man was more apparent as he towered overhead. There was a pinch in her neck muscles as she tilted her head a little higher to keep her gaze on his face. Fighting the flight response, she held herself steady.

Her throat went dry and her palms went wet, but she didn't turn her face away from Ailig, though her eyes darted to Gregor. His look flicked from Elle to Nicco, then to the house. Elle sucked in a deep breath and pivoted on her heel. Without further protest, she followed Nicco to the house. She heard neither movement nor conversation behind her as she went, but she held her head high and walked confidently, ignoring the pain of the day's ride. Nicco sniggered by her side, but she looked neither back nor at him as they left Gregor and the three tribesmen.

Many Meetings

Gregor Phillary
Phillary Vineyard
Tienne h'Ìosal, Caetera
16 de Lares, c.3683

THE FEELING OF BEING short was unfamiliar to Gregor. He stood as tall as possible amidst Ailig and his geàrden sa h-ain, watching the wards of House Phillary fade into silhouette as they approached the house. He had his work cut out for him with Elle, but that was a problem for the morrow. He turned and peered up to his Suebhian friend.

Ailig watched after Elle and Niccolai as well, wearing a pensive look. "Fire burns in her, mo bràthair khàinn."

"'Tis truth you speak, brother," replied Gregor. "I know the Suebhi do not experience our gifts, but hers is similar to my own."

Ailig raised both of his double brows and waved his guards away. "I still no like the boy."

"I have good reason to trust him. Can you bear his presence for my sake?"

"Jha." Ailig nodded. "Mo khinde, Màiri to manage with him."

Gregor clapped Ailig's shoulder. "You delegate well, Dion'Mor. You received my letter, I take it?"

Ailig peered down with only his eyes. "What need yer Dia'Mor?" he asked bitterly.

The Dion'Mor's respectful reference to Gregor's lover brought a smile to his lips. Regina Edony, Vasílissa of Terrináe, would be flattered that Ailig referred to her with the honor implied in the title of Dia'Mor, though untrue. Gregor rubbed his beard, considering for a moment how different Terrináe would be if it were more a clan like Ailig's than a web of social politics. It would certainly have been a simpler prospect. But he supposed the politics themselves were the reasons the citizens of Terrináe considered themselves above the stahmen.

"Our culture is not tribal," said Gregor with a tinge of regret. "We do not have a Dia'Mor...or Dion'Mor. Our vasileía is mostly symbolic of the culture's belief in balance."

Ailig snorted. "Who to make decision?"

They'd been through the discussion many times before. It developed both their vocabulary in the others' languages. Tonight, Gregor was simply too tired for the rhetoric. The fire called to him. He quirked a brow and asked, "Old friend, I should greet your stahm. Shall we enjoy some brüen and the warmth of the faella-tienne?"

The grasses, deep gold in the day, were a muted blue-grey under the stars and the two moons, Iana and Liberius. Wispy blades rustled against Gregor's calves as they crossed to join the others. He deeply inhaled the tang that the grasses emitted—a smell he associated with his love of both Edony and this place. The odor itself was his pure delight. Simply being here, at his vineyard, on the edge of Tienne h'Iosal, eased his soul. But for this trip, he'd only have his Edony within his heart.

Gregor recovered from his fancy as they reached the fire. Ailig remained at Gregor's side as the stahm greeted Gregor one by one with a forearm clasp and hand on the opposite shoulder. The population gathered was but a portion of Ailig's stahm, though they ranked among the leader's most trusted. Gregor had met them all over the course of the cycles he'd befriended their chieftain. Màiri approached last. Gregor sank to a knee offering the customary respect due to the future Dia'Mor.

As the obeisance required, Gregor's gaze was trained toward his hand on the ground. Màiri reached a hand into his line of sight, and said, "Stand, Gregor. And be welcome." Her accent all but faded as she spoke Terrináe's tongue musically. Her time spent in Gregor's home had trained her voice well.

Gregor pulled her hand to his lips and brushed them gently across her knuckles. "How fares the lovely daughter of the Dion'Mor?" he asked.

Her eyes flitted to her father briefly before she answered, "All 'tis well. Many thanks."

One of Màiri's first guard approached with a large clay mug and offered the frothy brüen to Gregor. His mouth watered in anticipation, but he owed thanks to the geàrde'sa h-ain before he could accept the drink. He tilted his head forward, touching his forehead with the flat of his fingers, then moved his hand to his chin, then his heart. No words were necessary, but he added, "Moran dank, Lothar," and accepted the offering.

Lothar rejoined the others as Gregor drank in long gulps. When he'd had his initial fill, he sighed and wiped his mouth. Then, to Ailig, he said, "I do understand that you bring me the weaker cavali for use throughout my city. Your reasons are just. But Brüà, I ask you this time, have you a caval suited for one of my own household...stronger in spirit and more like Ashe?"

"Jha." He regarded his daughter and added, "Haize."

Eyes twinkling, Màiri smiled, clasping her hands together under her chin as if bringing her inner child's giddiness under control.

Alphiné's Duty

Cera d'Alphiné
Second Cavern Temple
Est Idris Mountain, Caetera
16 de Lares, c.3683

CERA STOOD IN HER new chamber at the Second Holy Unity's cavern temple entranced by the flame's tongue licking from the coals of a dying fire. The granite walls kept the rooms chilled even in Estate when days and nights were hot, and the immense quarters appropriated for the voteri swallowed the heat. Recently back from the Éhrosi Isles, she hadn't relished the thought of returning to Her Lady's domain and taking up the votara's mantle, but after all the peace and healing the Second Holy Unity had provided, the job presented itself as a calling rather than something she could turn away. She prayed now that Her Lady d'Alphiné would use her gently and that Alphinus would watch over her as she served the newest inductees.

The time was well past gloaming when Cera divested the rose gold clothes and ornaments of her position. She'd bathed in private spring baths. An amenity afforded the voteri of the Ennead, she shared the blessed baths with Devan, Votoro d'Alphinus, but he'd been tending a follower in need that evening, so she'd washed alone. Afterward, Cera had wrapped herself in a warm towel-lined robe, securing it at her waist, but leaving her dark hair loose and wet over one shoulder to dry. She waited for Devan by the fire. Preoccupied with thoughts of what she faced, she didn't notice when the clarets near her bed began to dim in the fading hour.

Induction the prior evening had brought her back to her time with Gregor, and a flood of remembered happiness warred with terror and depression. The entrant, Elle possessed a strong psychological Flare; that Gregor had chosen her complicated the duty Cera was to perform.

Devan entered her chamber, foretold by the rhythm his heels tapped on the stone. Cera ran a hand under her eye at a tickle—a tear strayed down her face. She composed herself and turned to greet her other half with a smile.

"Mia bella," Devan proclaimed and held his arms wide as he approached.

Cera fell into his arms and the comfort he offered by the will of Alphinus. When she had accepted the appointment, they'd been joined in Unity for all time. This man had become her foundation, the one with whom she had shared the strife she had born, and without words, he offered her strength.

Pulling back, he looked into her eyes. Devan also possessed a psychological Flare, but not strong enough for much telepathy. His talent was more like intuition. There were times when he could project one or two words, but it was rare. More often, communication was through his wonderfully commanding words. "I see you have already bathed, but you will join me for a late soak."

Cera didn't mind his dominance. In fact, it relieved the burden of making decisions. She understood that his commands were always subject to her agreement, but to keep all things in balance, 'twas she who possessed the stronger Flare...she projected: *'I will.'*

Nodding, she noticed dark circles beneath Devan's eyes. While he comforted her, he'd also had a tiresome day. She could do naught but offer him the same solace.

Kurkuma Extract

Elle sur Phillary
Phillary Vineyard
Tienne h'Ìosal, Caetera
17 de Lares, c.3683

WAKING IN HER UPSTAIRS bedroom, Elle stared at an uninteresting ceiling. The dawn's light brightened the surface to a creamy white—a seemingly blank canvas awaiting an artist's brush. Is that what she was? What Braeden, Sonia, the others were? Blank canvases? That is what she had been led to believe from Yster's introduction to Terrináe. After induction though. nothing had been what she'd expected. She found herself wondering if it was possible that her choice to stay in Caetera had been the wrong one.

Stop it, Elle. You know second guessing yourself is just a waste.

She flipped onto her other side. Gregor was yet another puzzle. He seemed driven—to have other purposes. Then, as if she didn't have enough on the brain with figuring out her strange benefactor's agenda, she factored in the large, ominous tribesmen, a new language, and apparently a caval she had to learn to ride. Moreover, she probably should find some way to deal with her only—very brooding—peer.

At the frustrating thought of Nicco, Elle groaned and threw the covers off. Muscles and joints from her waist down protested with painful rigidity as she struggled to sit upright. Her arms didn't ache. For that, she could be grateful, but long hours in the saddle the day before did her little good. With careful movement, she searched the dresser for other clothes. Opening the third and final empty drawer, she slammed it shut. All she had were the clothes on my back. *That's just fantastic. Even if I can get a bath, I'll still smell like one of those damn cat-eyed horses—or cavali.*

Coffee. Maybe coffee would make the morning somewhat friendlier.

She emerged from her—hopefully, temporary—bedroom to head downstairs. Nicco mentioned school starting, so she assumed they'd be returning to Terrináe.

Gingerly padding the length of the hall, she ducked into the toilet room. Damn. Just sitting made her ass hurt! When finished, she made her way to the stairs and winced with each lowering step until she reached the ground floor. The wood creaked beneath her feet as she walked along the staircase past empty, dark-wooded rooms. The scene was reminiscent of Gregor's office and den in Terrináe. At last, when she turned and passed under the stairs at the rear of the house, she discovered the kitchen.

Her eyes and mouth widened as she marveled at the height of the ceilings—inconsistently vast in comparison to the rest of the house. She wondered if something about the cooking required a more open space. The wood silenced as she stepped onto stone floors. She felt like a child in an adult's kitchen where the counters rose to her mid-chest. Suddenly she wondered if this *was* Gregor's house. Though she couldn't imagine him working in a kitchen.

Shaking off her discomfiture, she crossed the room. Stoneware cups, a carafe, and a bowl with brown grounds sat alone on an otherwise empty counter. A quick sniff of the grounds confirmed that it was at least similar to coffee. Hopefully, it contained caffeine.

Elle pressed her brows together and pursed her lips in search of an automatic drip or, preferably, the instant gratification of a K-Cup. But she was sorely disappointed to find none. In fact, there weren't *any* appliances. Frustrated, she dropped the bowl back onto the counter with a clatter.

How the hell can I make coffee in this kitchen?

She reached for the pot. Heat radiated, and it sloshed heavily when she lifted it by the handle. When she poured, steam rose, and the liquid flowed brown. Tension drained from her shoulders at the happy resolution. Elle dipped her small finger into the carafe's white liquid and tasted. There was a slight unfamiliar sharpness, but it was cream—probably from some other unfamiliar beast. She added a swirl to her cup and limped to the table by the window. The chair height was almost that of a barstool.

You can do it, Elle. Just breathe through the pain.

Stiffly, she climbed into the chair and turned her attention to the glorious caffeine. She sipped the warmth and closed her eyes, letting it linger on her tongue before swallowing.

The coffee wasn't bad. Lazily, Elle opened her eyes and stared out the window. A ring of ash sat in the center of a circle of tents—three very large, hide-clad tents.

"Hi."

Elle jumped at the punctuated masculine voice. Coffee splashed onto her hand. “Ow!”

As he walked by, Elle briefly caught a smirk on Nicco’s face. He easily strode to the counter and poured his own cup. Frustrating man!

‘Couldn’t you even act a bit sore?’

Nicco smiled into his cup, then turned to Elle. “Ready for today’s lessons?” he asked, leaning against the counter.

With nothing to dry her hand, Elle licked the spilled coffee from her finger, eyeing him sideways with dropped brows. *‘Seriously, do I look ready?’* she thought.

Nicco quirked a brow, but Elle couldn’t figure out what would be so amusing. Silently, he watched her and waited.

In the end, she suppressed her snarky remark, if only a little. “You’re quite talkative this morning. Four whole words. To what do I owe the pleasure?”

He shrugged.

“You prove my point,” Elle mumbled and returned her attention to the scene outside. Behind the tents sitting on the golden grasses, grapevines stretched into the foothills. The peaks scraped the clear tanzanite sky in the distance.

Elle stared at it intently, hoping that Nicco wouldn't ruin it. She was too blasted tired this morning.

"Come." He exited the kitchen.

She didn't move. Keeping her voice at a volume appropriate to an audience only within the room, she responded evenly to his demand. "If you ask, I might consider the request." Whether he heard, she didn't care. She planned to enjoy her coffee and after, she would explore—alone if she must.

There was no movement outside the window, save for the gentle sway of the vines and an occasional lift to one of the tent flaps. The only interruption to the silence was the groan of the wood under Nicco's heavy-heeled footfalls, then the door slamming shut as he exited the house. Elle rolled her eyes and continued to sip.

Before long, the door shutting sounded again—softer. Elle looked toward the kitchen entry and waited. It surprised her that he'd returned.

In his place, a very tall woman stooped beneath the top of the door then rose to her full height. Elle placed the coffee slowly back onto the table.

Her eyes were large and deep ocher beneath double brows. Elle squinted, doing a double-take. Yes, she had four eyebrows, two over each eye. Elle pursed her lips, thinking of the night before. It had been too dark to make out if the men possessed the same feature. The young woman's hairstyle reminded her of Ailig and his guards, but she had far fewer markings—one blue circle on each jaw just below each earlobe. The purpose of the high ceilings and oversized furniture became clear. She wore soft tanned leather—a fitted halter baring her midriff, tight leggings, and boots covering calves more than twice the length of Elle's own. The likewise excessive lengths of her arms were bare.

"Elle?" The woman paused by the door. Her demeanor was matter-of-fact, but something about her amber eyes was open and inviting. "Your caval, Haize, is ready." She spoke with a slight Suebhian guttural softer than Ailig's.

"*My* caval?" Elle asked before remembering that it was one of the reasons they'd made the trip to the vineyard. "Ready for what?"

"A marcahd." The woman must have interpreted Elle's blank expression correctly, because she added, "the morning ride."

"I am sure you have the best of intentions but riding today is the last thing I want to do." Elle didn't believe her body could handle the torture. She shied away from the thought of climbing the ladder into a saddle. Then...the jarring, rocking, and constant straddled position. She closed her eyes and groaned.

The woman welcomed herself to sit at the table across from Elle, having no trouble with the height of the chair. She smiled in a warm greeting. "It is unfair that I have your name, but you do not have mine. Are you curious?"

"Give me a few days' rest, then I'll be curious. Right now, I'm saddle sore and spent from the full day of riding yesterday. The fact that you want me to get back onto one of those godforsaken beasts reduces my curiosity significantly." Elle smiled weakly, realizing late that her words were sharper than intended. Closing her eyes again, she inhaled, centered herself, and opened her eyes as she let out a long exhale. "I'm sorry. I don't mean to be rude. I've just been through a lot... Since you've mentioned it, you are?"

The young woman smiled, revealing two lines of straight white teeth. "I am Màiri of the Suebhi. Have you ever heard the saying, *return to ride and ride again*?"

"Is that like getting back on the horse?"

Màiri winced. "One might say that, but I beg of you, do not use the word horse in the presence of my people."

Elle remembered Ailig's words from the night before: *Hairse is bad word to my blood.* "I'm very sorry," she said running a finger around the rim of the mug.

She tilted the cup, looked at the little remaining, and considering she had nothing to lose, she asked, "Màiri, tell me, how do you come to be here, in this place? Er...in this world? Do you come from another plane or dimension, too?"

Her perfectly arched golden brows pulled together. "What do you mean? I came with my athair, Ailig. You met him when you arrived last night."

Elle sat up in the chair ignoring her protesting back and leaned toward Màiri. "Ailig is your father? Are you telling me that you were born here, in Caetera?"

She laughed at the question. "Oh...you are very, very new."

"No need to remind me." Elle finished the coffee, all too aware of how new she really was, and slid from the chair for a refill. Her back protested and standing up straight from the seated position was slow. Elle grunted and rubbed the muscles then hobbled to the counter for more coffee.

"I will return." Màiri disappeared into a small door on the non-entry side of the kitchen. After some shuffling, she returned with another cup, which she handed to Elle.

The cup held an orange, slightly foamy liquid. Elle sniffed, but it was odorless. She looked up to question Màiri about what it was she offered.

"It will help with the stiff muscles," Màiri answered, sitting back at the table.

Elle sipped the promised relief, and a shiver of revulsion at the bitter-sour powdery taste ran through her. There was no more than an ounce in the cup, so she threw it back quickly and washed it down with the coffee. She returned to the seat at the table, smacking her tongue against the roof of her mouth in a feeble attempt to eliminate the taste.

"Tastes like caval dung, but you will feel better before long," the Suebhian said. "As far as being born here, you will learn about this in your first cycle at school, but we..." She swung her finger in a vague pointing motion between the two of them. "I mean to say; you and I are not the same."

"Well...duh...you're tall, blonde, and a definite outdoorswoman. Me, well, standing next to you makes me look like a dwarf with red hair." Elle flipped the ends. "And I'm all city girl."

“That’s not what I mean.” Màiri ran a fingernail across the grain in the table. “We cannot...uh...breed with your people.”

The thought bent Elle’s brain in new ways. Màiri, Ailig, the others appeared human-ish, albeit very tall and with a second brow. But still—humanoid. Elle turned her head slightly as she leaned forward—unsure if she understood correctly. “You mean that we are entirely different species? Like our DNA is not compatible? Like...” Elle shifted her eyes in search of an example. Dogs and cats came to mind, but she didn’t know if those existed in Caetera. She snapped her fingers and said. “Like you’re cavali and we’re wapititos?”

Màiri shrugged one shoulder to her ear. “I don’t know about this species or DNA you speak of, but what you’re thinking seems right. My people did not suffer the loss from the plague or any of the ongoing effects.”

“Then what *are* you?”

The look Màiri shot Elle could have caused the house to go up in flames.

The heat landed in Elle’s cheeks as she once again realized how that must’ve sounded. “Uh... I’m sorry. I don’t mean to offend.”

After that, they sat in awkward silence for some time while Elle finished her second cup of coffee. Every few moments, she looked up to try and inspect some other feature of Màiri's that might give clues to differences, but outside of height and brows, she came up empty.

Màiri stared stoically through the window, not acknowledging Elle's surreptitious inspections. When the coffee was done, she asked, "How do your muscles feel?"

Elle slid off the chair to test the stiffness. There was still a dull ache, but it was tolerable now. Her eyes widened and her voice pitched. "What was in that drink?"

"Kurkuma extract. You look ready." Màiri stood, her eyes daring Elle to come up with another excuse.

Elle smiled, one that she didn't truly feel inside. "Fine, but only if you promise to make me another one of those nasty drinks when we get back. It makes a *world* of difference."

The intensity of Màiri's look didn't falter, and she made no reply. In the awkward silence, Elle turned and headed through the kitchen toward the door.

Cavali Cengal

Elle sur Phillary
Phillary Vineyard
Tienne h'Ìosal, Caetera
17 de Lares, c.3683

OUTSIDE, NICCO STOOD AMIDST a trio of cavali. He said something to Màiri in her own language.

Elle stopped with arms crossed over her chest. Indignant though it may have been, she was still annoyed with Nicco, and his use of a language he knew she couldn't understand stung. "It's unfair for you to talk in a language I don't understand."

Nicco's gaze shifted to Elle, and Màiri turned. Elle dropped her arms, understanding that the pose and the unfair comment painted her as a petulant child.

Nicco sneered. "As Gregor said, you *will* want to learn. Suebhian is preferred here." He motioned to the open air, presumably indicating the plains, or maybe just the vineyard. Elle was unsure.

“The Suebhi normally do not speak your language,” said Màiri, not kindly, but Elle accepted the information from her more readily. Chagrin dulled her edge. It was now apparent that Nicco had been simply showing her the respect that was due.

“I'm sorry.” *‘Again,’* she added silently. God, she hated being wrong and admitting it even more. “I didn't mean to offend. You and Ailig both speak English so well.”

The Suebhian woman patted her on the shoulder. Elle sensed that the gesture was to put her at ease, but it only made her feel smaller. Màiri explained, “I am the next Dìa'Mòr. To lead the tribe, you must have the languages.”

“Languages? Plural?” *‘Oh...that is just fabulous.’* Elle looked at the ground and rolled her eyes.

Màiri led the way to the waiting cavali. She scratched the animal under its massive jaw and extended a hand to Elle. Reluctantly, Elle followed, then slowly placed a hand in Màiri's. Her shoulders relaxed a little, not from anything unnatural, but the ease that came with feeling a blissful nothing at the touch. No calming effects. No buzzing. Just a touch. Màiri placed Elle's hand on the caval's velveteen muzzle. Upon contact, warmth infused her body, and affection replaced trepidation. Elle no longer feared to ride the beast, but, suddenly, this was no longer *a beast.* She—Haize—had such deep and specific feeling.

The world, and Elle along with it, stopped for the beat of a heart. She gulped to regain air stolen from her lungs. Breath reenergized her blood, and she searched the Suebhian's liquid amber eyes.

Màiri nodded, seeming to know the experience. "Yes. Feel the bond." She stroked Haize's neck and watched Elle, smiling warmly. "She likes you, and she claims you. The Suebhi call it cengal."

Sing-al, Elle repeated in her head…*as if she sings.* Elle's gaze had fallen back to where her hand rested on Haize's muzzle. She jerked her eyes back to Màiri's. "What do you mean—claims me? And can you spell that?"

"Nicco has your book. I will show you at the pond." The smile she wore showed just how deeply Màiri's admiration for these creatures ran. "Cavali are very particular about their riders. If she didn't approve, she would rear up, back away, and not allow you to ride her."

"If that's so, how did I ride Misty all day yesterday?" Elle asked, glancing toward Nicco.

"Because of me," Nicco answered absently. He didn't even look up from where he adjusted Haize's saddle and stirrups.

"Okay, fine," Elle said to Nicco. She may have been in the wrong about his use of Suebhian, but she still wasn't feeling friendly toward him. She turned back to Màiri, "I know nothing about animals. Yesterday was the first time I spent any time on the back of a horse, er...caval. Sorry that I keep interchanging the words."

"Haize will help to teach you," Màiri said, lovingly petting Haize's neck.

If she wouldn't allow someone else to ride, it didn't make sense that she was so amicable toward Mairi. "Do they claim more than one person? She sure seems to like you, too."

"No, they claim one and only one. But they are gentle. She knows that I will ride Nebiel." Màiri walked over to her own caval. "He claimed me as a young Suebhita before I could even walk. Haize has been untouched by any who were unclaimed. That made her eager to claim you."

Elle pulled down a six-runged ladder from Haize's saddle. Màiri's ladder was a short three rungs. With two steps she swung her long leg over to straddle her caval. Elle had climbed up yesterday, but always with help. This time she was on her own. She stopped and calculated which foot to begin with so that she didn't end up facing the hindquarters of her own caval.

Once mounted, she pulled the ladder up and stowed it across the long silvery-white neck in front of the saddle. Then, Elle swept a hand down Haize's neck, feeling a sense of pride that she had succeeded in mounting on her first attempt. She held certainty that the pride wasn't her own. Retracting her hand slowly from the caval's neck, Elle looked questioningly at Màiri and Nicco, wondering if she appeared as crazy as she felt. Maybe it was in her head. Nicco's smile seemed mocking while Màiri's was reassuring.

Màiri began the riding instruction, "You can press gently with one of your knees to have her turn toward that knee. To start her walking, squeeze both knees gently."

They walked the cavali away from the house, vines, and mountains and into a sea of grasses, allowing them to travel at an easy pace. Elle was told that she would become accustomed to the feel of riding solo. After what must have been an hour or more and the lulling started anew, Màiri—having circled her caval—trotted up beside Elle on Nebiel.

"How does it feel?" she asked, looking more natural atop the animal than Elle could hope for herself.

"This steady rocking may send me to sleep soon."

"Very well, if you're comfortable enough that sleep is possible, it is time for khav-astahr tienne." When Elle looked at her sideways, she added, "Cavali flight."

"Flight? Like last night?" Elle's heart thumped, and her mind raced to recall what Nicco did as Misty shifted into that gait. It all had happened so fast. All Elle could remember was his strong arm around her waist lifting her from the saddle. What if she was bounced off? "I...um... don't think—uh—I'm ready for that."

Looking across to Nicco who had slowed to their sides, he gave one short nod in answer to Elle's questioning gaze. Her eyes darted from Màiri to the ground far below where she sat atop Haize. She'd surely fall doing this alone. Elle shook her head in quick small motions.

"Haize will take care of you," Màiri said, then she touched her caval's neck. "Nebiel will lead, Misty and Haize will follow. Hold the reins here." She demonstrated.

When Elle mimicked her display, she continued, "Then stand in the stirrups in a crouch. This will brace you against the rough beginning and end."

Elle's thighs only protested a little when she stood, but she got it and nodded.

"Ready?" Màiri asked.

"No. Wait." Elle sat back into the saddle and breathed deep, remembering the feel of the gusting gait from before. "But it felt like we were rising and falling opposite of Misty's gait when we did this last night. Isn't there more to it than hovering over the saddle?"

Nicco laughed. "Nah...just feels that way."

Elle held her focus on Màiri, happy that she was successful not to even twitch in his direction. The manner in which he seemed to enjoy her pain this morning still had her annoyed, and she didn't need the insult of his laughing at her ignorance now. She had every right to ask these questions.

Màiri seemed to sense Elle's irritation and barked something sharply at Nicco in Suebhian. In a gentler tone to Elle, she added, "That is an illusion that you sensed. The caval's back rises and falls under you, but yer job is to keep yer legs as still as possible. Once the gait levels, you can relax in the saddle. We will approach a grove of trees, and I will signal like this to stop." She held her arm at ninety degrees with her hand fisted toward the sky. "When you see my signal, begin hovering again."

Elle did as Màiri instructed, and they were are soon past the bumpy beginning of the ride. The wind flowed through Elle's hair as they cruised across the grassy plains. In her hover, she was weightless and carefree.

Haize followed close behind Nebiel. His body worked beneath his rider, lean muscles contracting and releasing under the shimmering white coat. His head leaned forward, level with his back as did Haize's and Misty's. Presumably, this added to the animal's aerodynamics.

Màiri leaned forward in the saddle, looking intently in the direction they traveled. Elle tried to imitate her pose. Gazing off in the distance, she saw a copse of trees, growing closer. Then the wind took her breath away, and she let go of the uncertainty at being in yet another new place, the frustration with Nicco. For the first time she could remember, she had nothing to worry over, no job, no dates, no deadlines, no work obligations. She was unnaturally free. Her eyes prickled.

Màiri raised her fist. Elle blinked away the emotion and quickly attempted to shift her mental gears and grab the reins. She pushed with both feet against the stirrups to hover above the saddle, but too slowly. The saddle jarred into her lower back just before she could lift into the crouch, but her outcry was swallowed by the sound of the still rushing wind and slowing hoofbeats. That was a mistake she wouldn't make again. She rubbed her lower back as Haize came to a stop at the edge of the trees.

Maybe one day she'd learn the graceful leap from the back of Haize that both Nicco and Màiri performed, but today, she climbed carefully down the ladder. With both feet on the ground, she tucked away the ladder and stepped to Haize's head. Placing her hand on the muzzle, Elle first felt the sheen of sweat followed by a warm wave washing through her chest...happiness? Haize's happiness? Haize closed her eyes and, if it was possible, smiled as she leaned into Elle's caress. Before this connection, Elle had never imagined that animal feelings could be so reminiscent of her own swells of pride in accomplishment. She could never have dreamed that pure joy would defy gravity the same way for her and her beast. Elle rested her forehead on Haize's neck, basking in the utter humanity of the caval's pleasure.

"Bring her to the pond for water," Màiri called out, pulling Elle from her musing.

"Wow!" Elle said to Màiri as they approached the pool.

Misty was drinking alongside Nebiel and Nicco sat on the far side of the water. That was just as well. She could do without his brooding. Màiri brushed her caval as he drank.

"The cavali flight is unique to Tienne h'Ìosal. There is no other place on Caetera where that happens. And yes, wow!" Màiri handed over the brush.

Elle held it for a moment before taking it to Haize. How could she ask about the emotion? Lifting the dark bristles to the silvery coat, she asked, "Does Haize feel..."

Comprehension crossed Màiri's face, sparked in her eyes. Elle sighed with relief that she wasn't imagining such things. Màiri pinned Elle with her amber eyes and a bright smile. "That is your connection. *Cengal.*"

The Meeting, Part 1

Elle sur Phillary
Phillary Vineyard
Tienne h'Ìosal, Caetera
17 de Lares, c.3683

WHILE AT THE POND, Màiri and Nicco had drilled Elle in Suebhian such that her mind had been pushed beyond its bounds. Màiri had also provided instruction in the obeisance customs amongst the tribes of the plains. The deep bow due to the Dion— and Dia'Mor of each stahm was the most complex, but the first guards to each tribal leader were due the respect of a three-pointed head dip—touching the forehead, chin, and chest.

The return trip was easier, but by the time they rode up to the vineyard, Elle was craving one of Màiri's nasty orange shots. The camp was more active than when they'd departed in the morning; people milled around preparing for the evening's boar roast. Just outside the ring of tents, smoke rolled from the ground, thickening the air with the aroma of roasting meat. Elle's mouth flooded, and her stomach roared.

In the stables, Màiri handed Nebiel over to a Suebhian man, obviously still growing into his own skin. He was shorter than Màiri and awkward in his movements. He had no visible blue markings and wore his hair loose rather than in the high, wrapped tail worn by Ailig, his guards, and Màiri.

"Ar vaschen, Lyall." Màiri greeted him in the informal Suebhian.

Elle wondered, as she passed Haize's reins over, if the tail and tattoos were rights gained with age. Lyall accepted Haize, and Elle trailed her hand down the long white side as her caval was led away. She watched after Haize for a moment before turning to follow Màiri back into the house, unsure if the pang of sadness was Haize's or her own.

In the kitchen, Sirena sat on one of the high chairs, chopping vegetables at the counter. She was no taller than Elle, so the chair put her at the appropriate working height in relation to the counter. She didn't look up from her work as the two entered, so Elle presumed she was accustomed to comings and goings. Elle herself was immediately, desperately focused on relieving the aches and pains that had returned with a vengeance.

She leaned on the table while Màiri disappeared through the small door as she had in the morning and returned with the liquid relief. Elle sighed in anticipation and accepted the medicinal drink. Wincing at the taste, her voice cracked as she greeted Gregor's housemaid. "Hi, Sirena."

She paused in her work and turned smiling eyes to the greeting. "Happy gloaming to you, Mistress Elle," said Sirena.

Everything that Elle would imagine in a caretaker's kindness and deference was present in her look. Elle swallowed the lump in her throat as an image of Alvita, her assistant back in Corporate America, swam before her eyes. She blinked away the thought and shook away the absence of one of the only people she trusted. In Elle's shocked silence, Sirena had returned to her work.

"Just Elle," Elle said quietly.

"Pardon?" Sirena asked.

"You don't need to use a title with me. It's just Elle. When did you arrive?"

Sirena slid the last of the vegetables into a bowl. "Oh, I came just after first trivium. Had to take the long trail with the wagon to bring supplies. Give me a minute to get this cleaned up, and we'll go upstairs to get you prepared for the evening. There should be a bath cooling already, and your clothes are waiting."

'A bath and clean clothes? Heaven awaits!' Well, that may have been extreme, but it was music to Elle's ears. She had to be happy with something here.

"I'll see you tonight, Elle." Màiri excused herself.

Alone, in the kitchen, with Sirena, Elle wondered what she might learn about her benefactor from the sweet, older woman. "How long have you worked for Gregor?" she asked.

"Oh dear. I have been a Keeper at Phillary house since before Master Gregor inherited the position. Let's see, that was about two hundred and forty cycles back." She looked up from her work briefly, then added, "You'd call that about a hundred and thirty years."

Elle's jaw dropped. She'd been expecting forty, maybe fifty years, but more than a hundred? Damn. Those numbers left her speechless.

Sirena lined up the bowls on the counter, wiped down her working area, and dried her hands. To Elle's surprise, she hopped spryly from the chair and dragged it back to the table.

Elle smiled. Longer-lived indeed.

"Shall we? I'll go draw your bath. Meet me upstairs." The Keeper scurried through the door and turned toward the stairs, not waiting for Elle to follow. The steps creaked as Sirena climbed.

As Elle started up the hall toward the front of the house, a bark of a Suebhian command stopped her in her tracks. The voice was familiar from the prior evening, and Elle flattened herself against the wall.

Ailig slid in through the open front door, hunching to fit under the lower ceilings in the front of the house. His two guards stood with their backs to the windows on either side of the door. The tribe leader passed into the office on the other side of the stairs, just out of Elle's line of sight. A thump and click echoed off the wood as the office door closed. Looking around, it appeared that she was alone, so she tiptoed toward the stairs as silently as possible.

Deep voices carried through the door and office walls. They were thinner than she would have expected, and the language spoken was her own. Elle crept closer to clarify the conversation. Was this the important business they had come to conduct?

"Ailig, 'tis so good to visit with you and your stahm." There was a long pause. "But...you are aware that I am here on behalf of Regina Edony?"

There was no reply, but a pause, and glass clinking. She imagined Ailig nodded his understanding while one of the two men poured a drink. Then Gregor switched to Suebhian. Elle smothered a curse at not being able to follow the words, but how could she expect more after a single day's lessons?

"No," Ailig interrupted. "Terrináe's tongue—just to be sure. My men are outside."

'Yes!' Elle looked up as if to thank the gods—whatever gods there were.

"Very well...do you recall our time at the market?"

"Jha?"

"The young woman. The blonde that Sigrün had at the market. She didn't choose to be here. Edony wishes your help in discovering why she is and in making sure Terrinians are not enslaved by the tribes." Gregor continued.

Slaves? But this place was so...peaceful. Elle scratched behind her ear absently trying to reconcile how slaves fit into her Aveda underworld dream. If Ailig held slaves in his camp, there had been no indication. In the wake of Gregor's request, a long silence hovered. Without knowing Ailig better, Elle failed to imagine how he received the news.

At length, he replied evenly, "T'will be difficult to ask the Mor der stahmen."

"I understand. I only ask that you consider bringing this to the tribunal at the start of the cooling season. We realize –"

A hand clamped over Elle's mouth and an arm grappled her waist. *'What? Who?'* She tried to pry the grip from her mouth, but it didn't move. She kicked, but the strong grip dragged her from the spying post. She twisted and struggled, missing the last of Gregor's words. Defeat, setback, and sheer ire overcame her as she was pulled toward the back door.

The hand released her mouth, landing quickly on one shoulder. It spun her in a strong about-face and grabbed her arm. She realized it was Nicco, who snapped in a whisper, "You are lucky it is me and not one of Ailig's guards. The Suebhi sense of protection for their master is quite...extreme."

"I think that's the most words you've ever said to me at one time," Elle hissed and backed away, ashamed at her outburst and lack of discipline. She straightened her tunic. Self-control was something she'd trained into herself and her mind with every counseling session, with every bit of studying, and with every bit of exercise she'd undertaken. How was it now that anger and infuriation with Nicco just kept exploding? Though the ire had erupted and still flowed like lava, somewhere deep, she wondered if she was being too hard on the brute.

Nicco paused to look toward the front of the house, then continued, "Get upstairs. Get ready. Gregor wants to talk with you before the roast."

"Would you quit ordering me around?" She jerked free of his grip. It was far too close, familiar, and commanding. And now that she knew who had her, the humming had started up again where he'd held her arm.

They glared at one another, each daring the other to break eye contact. He no longer physically restrained her. It was only the standoff in each of their stares that paralyzed them both. Damnit, she was just about to learn something that actually seemed valuable. She was finally the one who broke the stare, bolting toward the office door, but his iron grip brought her to a halt. Fueled by fury, she snapped her head around to meet the anger that glowed in his blue-green eyes. Still conscious of the potential for getting caught, she kept her voice in a hush as she pressed Nicco, "They're talking about slavery. What's going on?"

"Not my place to know. Not my place to share. Go. Get. Ready." He pushed Elle toward the stairs.

She looked back at him. "Fine." She turned and climbed, not bothering to keep the footsteps silent. Her hands clenched and released as she went to her room. If Nicco winced at her heavy steps, good. If Gregor and Ailig heard, so be it. At least it wouldn't appear that she was spying on their conversation.

The Meeting, Part 2

Gregor Phillary
Phillary Vineyard
Tienne h'Ìosal, Caetera
17 de Lares, c.3683

HIS GUEST DUCKED THROUGH the door and Gregor stood to greet the Dion'Mor. Ailig cleared the ceilings when standing up straight, but just barely. Greetings exchanged in Suebhian, as the tribesman crossed the office, stopping at the bar.

"Ailig, 'tis so good to visit with you and your stahm." He felt more at home here, on the plains, with the Suebhi than he did at his home in Terrináe. But this meeting had another purpose. At the behest of his love. "But...you are aware that I am here on behalf of Regina Edony?"

Ailig poured a glass of Gregor's Armagnac and smelled. He closed his eyes and sighed at the heady aroma,

Gregor pleased that he took pleasure in the spirit produced at his vineyard. With a nod, Ailig crossed the room and took a seat on the chaise by the window. There wasn't a chance that he'd fit into one of the chairs in front of the desk.

In Suebhian, Gregor said, "There is a matter of slavery we need to discuss."

'Fuck!' The curse. Feminine. Elle. Harsh. Yet it trilled at his mind's ear. Gregor held up a hand and looked toward the door. His redheaded ward must be listening outside.

"No," Ailig replied. "Terrináe's tongue—just to be sure. My men are outside."

'Yes!' The trill came again.

Gregor extended a finger asking Ailig to wait while he called out mentally, *Niccolai, please come to the foyer and send Elle to prepare for the evening. She listens to a conversation she need not hear.*

He focused back on his immediate guest and continued, "Very well...do you recall our time at the market?" He couldn't help if she heard some of it. He'd simply have to choose his words with care until Niccolai arrived.

"Jha?" answered Ailig.

"The young woman. The blonde that Sigrün had at the market. She didn't choose to be here. Edony wishes your help in discovering why she is and making sure Terrinians are not..." He lowered his voice slightly. "...enslaved by the tribes."

Ailig drank, pausing for thought, then replied evenly, "T'will be difficult to ask the Mor der stahmen."

Gregor looked into his own glass. He'd needed the reinforcement to make such a request of his Suebhian friend. "I understand. I only ask that you consider bringing this to the tribunal at the start of the cooling season. We realize it will be difficult. 'Tis the reason behind the urgency of my missive. You will need the time to consider and plan."

He prayed that Ailig respected him enough that he would find a way to help. Otherwise, Gregor would have to find another way—a much *harder* way.

'What? Who?' trilled Elle's mental voice.

Gregor smiled. Niccolai had arrived.

"Yer drink. 'Tis funny?" Ailig asked, brows furrowed in confusion.

"No." Gregor sat back in his chair with a leg crossed and turned toward his Suebhian friend. "My newest ward, Elle. She is funny."

Ailig nodded and kicked his booted legs up onto the chaise. His mid-calf rested on the end, leaving his feet to dangle. He stared out the window into the sea of vines and into the Idris Mountains. "Jha, she has fire. Like mo khinde, Sorcha."

"Sorcha does have a fire within," said Gregor.

"How she to live in Terrináe?" asked Ailig.

"She fares well. She and her geàrden perform the Danssa Tienne each máda at The Whistle. It always draws a crowd." Gregor drank.

As he did, Elle's voice, hot with anger came back to him, *'Why does that man make you so angry, Elle?!'*

Gregor almost spat the Armagnac through his nose but stifled the laugh just in time. Obviously, Niccolai had arrived.

Ailig looked at him askew. In answer, Gregor shook his head while he recovered and wiped his watering eyes. "Anyway, my old friend. Will you help?"

DRAINING THE ARMAGNAC, AILIG considered his small brown-haired friend's request. Sigrün was his oldest friend, the blooded brother of his first love, and uncle to his first daughter. The request alone would offend. Gregor had demanded a great favor indeed, and one that Ailig was unsure he could accommodate. But with all they'd been through to come to this point, he would work to find a way to help a friend.

Difficult though it would be, Ailig's tribal blood was the oldest on the plains. Change was inevitable, and he possessed the most, the strongest influence. It was clear that without his assistance, Gregor would die trying to fulfill his lover's request. At length, Ailig answered, "Jha. I will."

"Moran dank," Gregor breathed and sat back into his chair. Turning subjects, he asked, "Will your Dannsair Tienne perform this night, after the feast?"

Flaming Plains

Elle sur Phillary
Phillary Vineyard
Tienne h'Ìosal, Caetera
17 de Lares, c.3683

ELLE SHOOK OFF HER annoyance and entered her room. Leaning her back against the closed door, her attention was drawn to a dull glow outside the window. She slowly crossed the room and raised a hand to her mouth, covering a long and silent gasp as she took the grasslands at sunset. The blades danced with reds, yellows, and oranges in the wind that brushed across the plains. It wasn't the same glow of the Noctilucent Clarets, but the sea of golden grass grabbed the fire from the sun and reflected it on its blades. Nicco's earlier explanation that the Flaming Plains were mere grasslands had been a most grave understatement. There was no smoke, but otherwise, the scene before Elle appeared as if a massive fire ravaged the land.

“Mistress. Is everything alright?” Serina asked from the door, having arrived on silent feet. Elle hadn’t heard the door open. When she turned with awe-filled eyes to the Keeper, Sirena smiled and corrected herself, “Er...Elle. Your bath is ready.”

Turning back briefly to the grasses dancing in the fading light, Elle wanted nothing more than to stand there until the dark had fully extinguished the flames if only to be certain that it was a trick of the light. But Gregor would be waiting and it seemed important that they meet before the evening’s festivities. Then there was the fact that she had been on a caval for two days straight. She shot Sirena a thin smile and joined her.

The Keeper led Elle silently into another room where a private bath was drawn, placed the towels on a chair, and left.

Every fiber of Elle’s body relaxed when the door closed, leaving her alone. Sinking into the water, her eyes closed, and her head rested on the tub. Long and slow breaths traveled in through her nose and out through her mouth. How many inhalations and exhalations passed in meditation, she didn’t know.

So far, the day's adventure had been a series of unexpected ups and downs. In the morning, she'd damn near questioned her choice to stay. Though had she chosen the flame, there would be no Haize. Her breath would not have been stolen by the Suebhian flight or that fiery sunset. While the mentors advertised Terrináe's utopia, Elle's choice to stay wasn't based on any intended delusions of grandeur. In fact, the lack of comfort had emphasized the wrongness that permeated her situation. It reinforced the reasons she chose the soil—the alternative felt *wrong*.

The thought of rising from the cocoon of warmth was unwelcome when a knock sounded at the door. "Your clothes for tonight are on your bed," Serina's voice informed Elle from the other side of the door. The night was improving: a bath *and* clean clothes. Elle smiled and exhaled, humming with satisfaction.

Turning to the business of bathing, she opened and carefully sniffed the contents of each bottle lining the shelf by the tub. Selecting the appropriate smells based on her bathhouse memories, she completed the routine. When finished, a quick search found no drain. She wrinkled her nose with a tug of regret for whoever must empty the dirty water.

With her hair and body wrapped in towels, Elle looked both ways in the hall to verify that she was alone, then padded quickly to her room. Time to dress and join the festivities.

The skirt on the bed was full and patterned in multi-colored patchwork, and there was a shorter, soft hide overskirt. Elle held up a leather bra and inspected the two embroidered triangles with lines of turquoise stones and the long leather strings.

'Strange bra,' she thought.

She looked for a shirt, but there were no other garments present. *'Marvelous.'* She rolled her eyes and sank onto the bed next to the costume.

'I am meant to parade around in the company of very large strangers in a bikini top and skirt.'

That wasn't her idea of a great party.

'And Yster told me I was indecent wearing pajamas.' Elle sighed and dressed.

She was fumbling with the long leather strings on the top when the door opened. Seeing Elle's frustration, Sirena dropped her load on the bed and rushed over to help. She wrapped the lengths around Elle's torso crossing in the back, then in front, then meeting at her waist in the back where she tied them off.

"Shoes?" Elle asked.

"There are no shoes for the traditional Suebhian feast attire."

"Can I wear the slippers anyway?" She wasn't accustomed to running around barefoot.

The look Sirena gave her was enough to say how insulting that would be, but she simply said, "Not a good idea. Have a seat."

Once Elle was in the chair facing a mirror, Sirena pulled her hair into a braid, tucked it into itself with a few pins and added a beaded headdress. The turquoise stone that rested at the center of Elle's forehead tickled. When she reached up to scratch, Sirena shooed away her hand and placed a clunky necklace resembling a bib around her neck. The adornments were harmonized between the necklace, headdress, and the bra-top.

Elle reached up and fingered the necklace and headdress. They were both lighter than their appearances. Touch and the mirror revealed that the stones were set, not in metal clasped with chains, but in the same pale tan leather as the bikini top.

"There, you're all set." Sirena clapped her hands at her work of art and beamed like a mother readying her daughter for the senior prom—not that Elle would know that feeling. She winced.

'Shake that off, Elle. It was a long time ago.'

To appear so proud of someone she barely knew, Sirena must be the motherly type by nature. Elle stood so that she could view more of herself in the mirror. Unfortunately, she didn't feel ready for a prom or any other formal affair. This tribal version of Elle was a far cry from the Elle who presented the quarterly report to a corporate board of directors only days, or maybe weeks, before.

Wait! Elle turned quickly, searching for the source of that memory. "Ho-ly-shit..." she said as vague flashes of the memory came to her. She couldn't see faces, but she knew her presentation by heart. "Travelers..." she breathed. But she had worked at Jewel Systems, right?

"Mistress? Are you alright? Should I get Master Phillary?" Sirena fussed over Elle.

It was enough to pull her from the daze. She looked up into the round, worried face. "I'm sorry." When were they going back to Terrináe? Elle pursed her lips. She had new business with Yster.

Smiling weakly at Sirena, she pushed the memory and the thoughts into a compartment for later. Standing and walking to the door, she grasped the doorknob, sighed, and pulled. "Showtime."

In the hall, she met Nicco who was repeating his performance from outside The Odeum the night of the induction ceremony. He sheathed the black-bladed knife and stood straight. A new look danced across his blue-green eyes as they traveled from Elle's headdress, to the floor, and back to her face. As if he had forgotten it was open, he closed his mouth, and his brows pressed downward. He hesitated, then wordlessly descended the stairs. His usual lack of words had been by his own choosing. This time, it seemed that Elle had forced his silence. A satisfied smile split her lips, and her bare feet followed him down the stairs.

Flare

Elle sur Phillary
Phillary Vineyard
Tienne h'Ìosal, Caetera
17 de Lares, c.3683

NICCO HELD THE DOOR to Gregor's office, allowing Elle to enter ahead of him. Behind her, his heels marked his entry followed by the snick of the door. Gregor sat relaxed on the other side of the tidy dark wood desk, Ailig no longer present. Both Gregor and Nicco were dressed identically in the male version of the Suebhian traditional attire. Their chests were bare under lightly-tanned leather vests adorned with the same turquoise stones that decorated Elle's costume.

"Thank you, Niccolai. That will be all."

An unnatural force colored Gregor's dismissal, so Elle turned to see Nicco nod obediently and retreat from the office, closing the door in his wake. If he was upset by the ordered discharge, there was no indication in his loafing exit. Elle chewed the inside of her lip, wondering what made him defer so to Gregor.

When she turned to the man in question, he rose and said, "I agree with you; he can be very frustrating."

"Agree with me?" Elle pursed her lips. "Interesting choice of words. What makes you believe I find him frustrating?"

Gregor didn't respond, but light flashed in his brown eyes. He smiled and approached the small table with bottles and glasses—similar to the setup in the front rooms in his home in Terrináe. Glass in hand, he poured himself another ounce of amber liquid. "Help yourself." He raised the drink toward the table.

Elle poured a glass of wine. Then without being told, she took a seat in front of Gregor's desk.

"No. Stand."

A flush of warmth rose through her neck to color her cheeks—the downside of being a redhead. Sufficiently chided, Elle slowly stood.

"Place the glass on the desk and demonstrate the expected obeisance suited for the Dion'Mor," he commanded.

'Some expectations? No. Shit.' "I thought—"

Gregor raised a hand to stop her protest. "Elle, these are my guests. In my home. Hospitality requires that I feed his tribe, but Ailig has broken with the sacred Suebhian custom and is hosting the boar-roast himself. I will be damn certain that no one in *my* household offends."

Elle placed the glass on the desk and stood to do as he demanded, thinking, *'And you wonder why Nicco is so disagreeable?'*

She performed the bow, falling to one knee and placing a hand on the ground.

Thinking twice about the barbs she wished to toss at her benefactor, she decided she needed to win over this man and said simply, "You know...I *can* be agreeable when asked nicely."

He placed a hand on her shoulder to make a minor correction to her posture. "Good. You may take your seat now." Skirting around, he took his own chair, propping his boots onto the corner of the desk.

'Thank you, Master.' Sarcasm dripped from Elle's inner voice.

"Happy to help...now, what questions do you have?"

Elle dropped her brows. *'Alright...he's definitely reading my mind.'* Slowly, uncertainly, she answered his question, "We can be here all night with the number of questions I have. How about you start with telling me what I can expect from school." That seemed to be a safe enough starter question.

He rolled his glass slowly back and forth between his palms. "T'will be an evaluation before school starts. After that, the results will be reviewed with myself, you, one of the instructors, and your mentor. Yster, true?"

"Yes. Do you know her?"

"I know her benefactor." Gregor cleared his throat and averted his eyes before adding, "Andreas Javine. But that's not important. How do you like Yster?"

"She's nice, I guess." Elle's forehead creased in that one place between the brows where she was sure she'd have a wrinkle when she was older. "Perfect really. Maybe too perfect? I don't really know her though. Will I spend more time with her?"

“It is her job to see you through induction and through your first cycle here. She won’t trail you everywhere like she did before, but you’ll see a great deal of her.”

Elle sipped the wine and got back to the original question. “Evaluation. What’s the purpose of that?”

“Ah...it will tell us about your Flare. Although, I am pretty sure I already know.” He raised a brow at her.

Elle furrowed her brow. “Alright, first, what’s a Flare? Then, maybe you could enlighten *me* on what it is you already know?”

“Everyone here has a Flare. Well, at least that’s true for everyone in the city. It’s how you were located and why you are here.” He dropped his feet and placed his empty glass on the desk, leaning forward onto both elbows.

His words were simply not falling into place. “I don’t follow,” she said.

“Let me provide examples...Yster and other mentors can calm your anxiety. That’s biological Flare.” He bored into Elle’s eyes with his own. *I can communicate without words.*

Elle stopped dead, glass halfway to her mouth. She could swear the sound actually tickled her ear. “What the hell? How did you...”

"Oh, come on Elle. This is not the first time I've talked to you that way. Think about it."

Returning her glass to the table in slow motion, her eyes dropped, searching, but not really seeing anything. Then she recalled. Her jaw gaped, her mouth forming a wide O. That first night...his manner of turning away on his last sentence...words...his words...in her mind. Elle inhaled and her eyes went round.

She looked up into his chocolate stare accusingly. "Is there more? Can you read my thoughts too?"

"I cannot pull your private thoughts from your mind."

Her shoulders relaxed a bit with that answer. "That doesn't quite answer my question, though."

"No. It's just like if I spoke the words." His words were casual as if this was an everyday conversation.

Maybe it was routine for him, but telepathic conversations—real mental communication—would be beyond anything Elle could imagine. That is...if it hadn't just happened. "Is this like cengal? With the cavali?"

A chuckle rumbled low in his chest. "Similar, but not precisely. You do put things together quite quickly."

"What about Nicco?"

Wheels were still turning, and the words spilled out even before the thought was even processed. She had been in close contact with him on the trip to the vineyard, and there had been no sense of anything mind reading. Though there was his special talent for non-conversation. And...that buzzing or humming when they touched. That must have been whatever his special condition was. Was it like a disease?

“Nicco’s Flare is physical. There are four major Flares.” He ticked them off on his fingers. “Psychological, me...physical, Nicco...biological, Yster...and chemical, Sirena. But you haven’t seen that yet.”

“So, this evaluation will tell me all about my own Flare. Then what?”

“All it will show is the major area of your Flare. The assessors may get a sense of a little more, but long practice is what really tells you the limits of your own Flare.” He sipped. “What else?”

“You didn’t answer my other question. What do you suspect is my Flare?”

“I’d like you to trust that I’ll discuss yours with you after the testing.”

"Okay..." said Elle. Trust wasn't very high on her list, but it was supposedly only a few days away. Time for a different question. "Why did you choose me? At Induction."

He sighed, then swallowed. "The answer to that question is directly related to the testing. I will have a better answer for you after the review."

'Damn. Strike three.' Elle nodded. He had to be able to give her some kind of answers. "What will I owe you for being my Benefactor after my schooling? What's the payback? Requittance, I think Nicco called it."

A rasping sound filled the silence as Gregor rubbed the stubble on his jawline. "I honestly don't have an answer for you or myself on that question. I don't typically take in entrants...can I get back to you?"

"Okay," she said, disappointed. She didn't really have a choice though—at least she didn't think so. Though it was oddly a bit endearing to know he didn't have all the answers. She finished her wine.

"My turn. Outside of this portfolio all about you..." He dropped a file on the desk. "Tell me about Elle. Who she is, what she enjoys, what she fears, what she hopes for..."

Fire Dance

Elle sur Phillary
Phillary Vineyard
Tienne h'Ìosal, Caetera
17 de Lares, c.3683

BEING OUTDOORS WAS A relief after reviewing the resumé that Elle had never submitted and going through an interview for which she was sorely ill-prepared. The fire of the plains in the sunset had been extinguished, and a new fire atop the black-scorched circle was now ablaze. Dual moons hung low in the sky, preparing to make their nightly climb.

Màiri was amongst the Suebhi of Ailig's party milling around the flames. She smiled as Gregor and Elle joined the festivities and waved Elle over while making some unheard commentary to her companions. Elle glanced up to Gregor seeking—what? Permission? His nod released her to join them. As she strolled toward the fire, Elle rolled her eyes at feeling childish for what seemed like the hundredth time that day.

Careful of the ground beneath her bare feet, she went to Màiri. Since the two Suebhi were of a height with Màiri, Elle stepped onto the log for a more comfortable vantage point. "I was beginning to feel that I was to be on display," said Elle, lifting her skirts. She was relieved that Màiri wore a similar outfit—the same bralette, but skirts in blues and greens.

"You are a sight to behold in our customary dress," Màiri said, then said something to her friends in Suebhian.

Elle tried to follow, but only caught about one in every five or so words. Studying the language was a must before she returned to the vineyard. Her forehead wrinkled at the thought. That was assuming she'd return and that they'd also be there. Dismissing the thought in the celebratory atmosphere of the gathering, Elle returned her focus to the trio.

Màiri turned and said, "Elle, this is Drostan and Lothar. Unfortunately, they do not speak your tongue."

"Ar vaschen d'ehrlichen," Elle said. It was getting easier. Then she whispered to Màiri, "Should I bow to them?"

"No." A soft, easy laugh followed her reply. "You can save that for if you're called in front of Athair."

"Aithar?" asked Elle, then the word clicked. "Oh, your father. Ailig."

It was easy to be around Màiri and her friends; there were no demands, and the foreign dialog allowed Elle's mind to wander. She mulled over her halting answers to Gregor's questions from before, which were very good. What *were* her hopes? She was no longer so sure of the answer, and the only hopes she could fathom were to understand more about this place, about the reasons she was here, and why the reason the others' decisions to return to their homes bothered her so. But the questions piled up...she now had to figure out whatever was meant by this Flare-thingy and what Gregor spoke with Ailig about. The tribes enslaved people from Terrináe? Looking around the fire, there were only the Suebhi and their party.

"Elle," Gregor called from behind where she stood.

She pivoted on the log, then lost her balance and stumbled. Recovering, she stood face-to-face with Ailig's rippling bare abs. Her mouth went dry. The leader's two guards, minus the staves, and her Benefactor were also there. Elle's cheeks glowed.

'Fucking wonderful. I really have become an awkward teenager,' she thought.

She was too close. Gregor grinned and reached to steady her as she hopped a step back so that craning her neck might be a bit less painful. Ailig's glare was steady and patient as he waited.

Elle lifted the skirts and crouched to perform the obeisance due to the Dion'Mor. She was thankful that the aches from long riding had mostly subsided. While she considered the formality of this particular custom seriously outdated, bowing to Ailig seemed *unnaturally* natural. Although, in the presence of the immense Suebhian, she did feel slightly like Alice after sipping from a bottle labeled *DRINK ME.*

She looked toward her hand on the ground, waiting to be released. The position was severely subservient in that she couldn't even see the person to whom she offered the obeisance. He might well do anything he wished to her at that moment, and she'd never see it coming. Under those thoughts, her pulse quickened, but then the giant hand entered her field of vision. She sighed and completed the ritual by touching her forehead to the ground and accepting the proffered arm. "Mòran dank," she thanked him as she rose.

Ailig held her forearm gently. "Sehr mhath."

Long study was necessary to follow deeper conversation, but Elle was pleased with the little bit of Suebhian she'd gained that allowed her to understand his acknowledgement of her thanks.

"Be at ease und enjoy the roast," he said, then released Elle's arm. He took a goblet from one of his men and handed it to Elle before he strode away. Before Ailig's first guard left, she also performed the three-pointed small bow to them as a unit.

'Well done.' Gregor's tenor swept against her mind's ear, and she tensed. That would be something to get used to.

Elle tilted her head to one side, following him with her eyes around the growing fire where a dozen, maybe more, Suebhi gathered. As he approached others, they offered him the same obeisance. Elle felt akin to Ailig's followers who instinctually deferred to this leader. She too sensed a primeval command in his presence. The feeling was unlike the respect that was owed to corporate officers or political leaders on Earth. It ran to a basic level within—a place that she rarely felt touched.

"He likes you." Màiri nudged Elle's arm. "He does not talk with many. Aithar talks with Gregor but refuses Nicco."

"Oh..." Elle, returning from her reverie, faced Màiri. "Why is that?" Lothar and Drostan were no longer there. She sipped from the goblet, the contents cold and creamy with a sharp taste of freshly baked bread and a warmth in the finish that blazed down her throat.

"I would imagine it's something to do with yer small Mor there." She held her own drink in Gregor's direction, then shrugged. "Doona know fer sure." Her guttural tone hadn't surfaced much earlier in the day. It was still mild as they talked, but slightly more pronounced. Màiri obviously had grown easier through the day and into the night, or she was getting drunk.

Elle looked up at her questioningly. "Màiri? How long has Ailig been the stahm leader?"

She looked up, then started to puzzle it out. "Well, Opa died about forty cycles back. That's when he took over."

"Opa?" asked Elle.

"Aithar's aithar," she replied.

"Were you around then?"

"Oh, jha." She looked pensively into her goblet. "And my sister too. But she no longer rides with our stahm," she said with a small rueful smile.

"Has she been gone long?" Elle asked, sensing some emptiness in her words, but unsure if Màiri meant she had also died or if she just left the tribe.

"She left in the second cycle after Opa crossed the long plains. We haven't seen her since." She ran a finger around the rim of her goblet. Then she quirked her mouth, shrugging off an invisible ghost.

"Why did she leave?" asked Elle.

"She didn't want the geblüt." Màiri looked up, then added, "That's the family duty to the stahm. It's inherited, and she's oldest."

"So, it's yours now?" Elle felt the tug of Màiri's sister's loss as well as her gained burden to this tribe—not to mention Ailig's very large shoes to fill.

Màiri nodded solemnly. Then, in an instant, her eyes widened, and a child-like grin broke across her face. "Grab some food, the fun's to start soon."

The meat from the boar was smoky rich and melted on Elle's tongue as they sat on the log, eating and waiting for the supposed fun to begin. The sun had long since ducked beneath the horizon, and the bonfire was the only light in the plains free of the Clarets. Two of the Suebhi dipped long torches into the fire, lighting both ends, then left fireside. Other tribesmen followed in groups of twos and threes.

Màiri took Elle's plate and grabbed her hand. "Come. 'Tis time."

Dropping the plates and empty goblets on a table, they went outside the ring of tents and into the dark beyond where the bonfire's light couldn't reach. Màiri's quick step and run toward the action was contagious. It was almost childish, like sneaking into a show that was forbidden to their age. Elle caught her breath when they came to a stop, trying to recall the last time she felt so light and carefree. The caval ride was a release, but this was almost giddy.

The Suebhi with torches gathered in a line. A drumbeat began, slow and steady, then quickened. From one end, the torches started to spin and twirl, setting circles of oranges and yellows ablaze in the darkness. As Elle absorbed the lights trailing from the torches, she caught herself tapping her toe to the beat of the drums and fought the urge to move.

At first, there was no pattern or consistency to the ghosts of light left by the torches, but soon a seemingly choreographed spectacle began. The Suebhi aligned, six wide, and the flaming swirls chased one another through the night.

The sequence progressed, and each of the six dancers tapped one end to the ground—then the other. The live flames faded to banked embers on the ends of the torches, then the twirlers resumed the dance. Speeding to the drums' increasing tempo, the torches sent sparks flying from the arcs of the poles. The embers sprayed and showered in the night sky in a dance more brilliant and continuous than fireworks.

The wine combined with whatever Suebhian drink was in that goblet loosened Elle's restraint. By the time the final beat sounded, she was twirling—actually dancing to the rhythms. She clapped with abandon, and a long yell of enthusiastic support escaped her throat.

She stood on her toes and stretched toward Màiri. "That was amazing!"

The words had scarcely left her mouth when the drumbeat began anew. One routine followed another, and as the show continued, Elle moved her entire body to the beat.

When the fire performance finished, the entire crowd filtered slowly back to the ring. Upon her arrival fireside, Elle was offered and accepted another of the goblets, wondering idly if it would cause a hangover in the morning. Choreographed movement started around the fire and put her in the mind of a Native American ghost, war, or sun dance. These, though, were partnered and a simplistic three-step repetition.

She finished her seconds of the rich Suebhian drink just before Gregor approached with a sly smile and offered his hand. Elle pulled away, recollecting the same motion at the induction ceremony. Although his demeanor now was not so demanding.

"Elle...would you like to join?" he asked, wearing a smile that colored his entire face. "I will show you."

In response to his uncharacteristically pleasant invitation, Elle accepted his hand, grateful that he spoke in voice and not in mind. Gregor, obviously experienced in this dance, positioned her in preparation. With his right arm around her waist and their left hands joined, he demonstrated the footwork while counting. Soon she could follow his lead, and they joined the others closer to the fire.

The only thing she felt at their touch was a sense of ease and belonging. Strangely, she mused that she could definitely grow to enjoy the company of this man.

Gregor continued leading Elle around the fire, marking time with the drumbeats. "It's nice to do this with someone who is not so tall." His breath was warm on Elle's ear. Unlike with Nicco, she felt no familiarity, no anxiety, no tension.

When the drums halted, Gregor released her, and Elle stumbled slightly. The flames of the fire multiplied and blurred before her eyes. She raised a hand to her head as if she could stop the spinning. "I think it might be time for bed."

Gregor steadied her with a hand beneath her elbow. "How much did you have?"

Certainly not enough to be drunk. "Only two glasses, plus the wine in your office." Elle's giggle betrayed her.

"It may be good to stick with one. The Suebhian brüen is quite strong." He walked her to the log and eased her to sitting, then disappeared.

With elbows propped on knees and head in her hands, Elle inhaled deeply, repeatedly forcing the air through her mouth, to keep the world from tilting. When Gregor returned, Sirena was by his side.

"Oh dear," she tsked. "Too much of the old brüen will surely give you the stumbles. Let's get you to your room."

Sirena looped her arm in Elle's and guided her away from the fire and into the house. Upstairs, she helped her get out of the costume and into a sleeping shift.

Elle was nestled cozily into the bed with drums and distant voices drifting up from the fire. The glow of the Noctilucent Clarets on the table waned into the deep of night, and she drifted until there was nothing more.

Journey Home

Gregor Phillary
Idris Vale, Caetera
18 de Lares, c.3683

THE RETURN TRIP WENT slow as the three on cavalback had grown to a caravan. Though Gregor was always eager to return to Edony, Vasílissa of Terrináe and his love, the pace was of little worry. Evaluation Máda didn't start for six iméri. Sirena drove the carriage, and the others rode. Gregor had traded a season's worth of Armagnac for the half dozen cavali Ailig offered. Having given Haize to Elle, he had five remaining for sale in Terrináe. It was well. The steeds commanded a nice price.

Lyall, Ailig's youngest son, had joined the group for the return trip and would serve Phillary House by tending to Gregor's cavali as well as the cavali around Terrináe. Part of Gregor's deal with Ailig was that the cavali were well tended. Gregor readily complied as he cared equally for the steeds. And the service Lyall provided to the others who owned cavali in Terrináe would bring in a sustained profit.

They stopped where the golden grasses turned green at the mouth of Idris Vale. After another of his Keeper's magical meals, they settled in for the night. Across the fire, Elle curled up inside Haize's legs. Gregor had also watched Elle over the course of the day's journey and it appeared she was taking well to her connection with the cavali. He rose to check in on her before he retired under the stars for the evening.

He deliberately rustled his boots as he approached and watched until she looked up. "I didn't want to frighten you," he said, offering Elle a blanket.

Cavali could be territorial, and Haize watched him warily with her glowing green eyes. He slowly placed a hand on her muzzle. *'Easy there, pretty girl. I mean you no harm,'* he projected. Cengal could only be formed between one caval and rider, and Gregor's was with Ashe, but it appeared that all caval could understand his projected thoughts. He'd always had a way with steeds—even the Lippizans he'd trained in Vienna's Spanish Riding School had been eased by his kind thoughts and a touch.

Haize's muscles tensed, then eased, and her eyes drifted to slits as Gregor stepped inside her protective circle and sat beside Elle. He sat by her side in silence for several moments, just enjoying the quiet.

"Gregor," she said.

"Hmmm?" He inclined his head in her direction.

"Some of the reason for this trip to the vineyard is apparent." *'How much does he know I overheard?'*

He knew she'd heard him touch on the enslaved Illaura but wouldn't acknowledge that just yet.

Elle pressed on with a vaguer question. "Were there reasons to visit outside of purchasing the cavali?"

"Shh," he said. *'There is a sense of peace at the fire, no?'* he added in mind. In his periphery, she tensed. *'Are you okay if I speak to you thus?'*

'No!' her mental voice trilled, but she paused and replied, "Yes."

He went with her voiced answer, still suspecting that she didn't know of her own telepathy. *'It won't be long, and I'll let you sleep.'* He smiled but didn't look from the fire. Shifting slightly to gain more comfort, he continued, *I recognize that you have more questions. 'Tis natural in your situation. I need more time though and the evaluation. Can you be patient with me?'*

'No! I want...I deserve to know more!' she shouted mentally. But again, she relented. "Yes, I believe I can."

He smiled, patted her leg, and rose to return to Ashe and his pallet. "Nicco has first watch, Lyall has second, and I have third. I'll wake you in the morning." Gregor skirted the fire and curled himself up inside the circle of Ashe's legs, pulling a blanket to his chin and closing his eyes.

Phillary House

Elle sur Phillary
Phillary House
Terrinae, Caetera
23 de Lares, c.3683

OVER THEIR SLOW RETURN, Elle slept better than anticipated on the hard ground encircled by Haize's legs. Throughout the trip, she'd learned a bit more Suebhian, and practiced with the new stable boy, Lyall. The process was slow as they each learned the other's language together. But to her disappointment, she learned no more from Gregor. By the time they arrived at Phillary House on the third day, Elle was in sore need of another bath.

She deposited her meager possessions—small enough to fit in a saddlebag slung over Haize's saddle—into her room in the upper corner of Phillary House. Looking at the bed longingly, she fought the urge to crawl inside and instead searched for someone who could direct her to where she could bathe.

Gregor's chocolate brown gaze looked up from his work as Elle entered the office. His countenance was all business—not at all the easy, yet commanding man she had glimpsed at the vineyard. There was no longer the amusement she'd felt in his gaze beside the fire as they'd danced. Perhaps her imagination fabricated that sense, or maybe he had been feeling the pull of the Suebhian brüen at the time.

"Where can I bathe?" Elle asked.

"Just up the hill. Before you pass the gates into the rest of the city, there is the benefactor's bath house." He turned to a shelf and retrieved a paper. "When you're done, go to the dressmaker. Out the gates and down the row to the right; third building on the left."

Elle unfolded the paper to see a bank note with the heading: *Traveler's Bank, Tesoreria de Terrinae* and *Account Holder: Gregor Phillary* across the top, his signature on the line at the bottom. *'Traveler's Bank—interesting.'* In her first days in Caetera, she'd forgotten, but her memories had been slowly returning. Travelers Companies was the name of the company she'd worked for back on Earth at the time she was taken.

"Lilliana," Gregor interrupted her train of thought, "the clothier, will fill out the amount and turn it into the bank for payment. Make sure you request school, riding, and formal clothes—all in my colors."

At the mention of his colors, Elle took notice of his clothes—a burgundy vest over a fitted tunic the color of slightly toasted biscuits, black pants, and black boots. She also recalled that Nicco wore the same burgundy and beige combination. She smiled sweetly and professionally and left him to his work. Those colors worked for Elle. Not as well as black, but at least they suited her autumn coloring far better than the grey of the entrant-wear that made up the lion's share of her current wardrobe.

She reached for the door to leave.

'Do not be too late. Evaluation tomorrow. You'll need your energy.'

Elle's whole body tensed, and she froze in place. Closing her eyes, she drew in a cleansing breath to shake off the invasion of Gregor's words. How long was it going to take to become accustomed to hearing a foreign voice in her own mind? It could make one believe they were developing a mental disorder. Maybe she was. Maybe this was all an elaborate hallucination still.

She threw open the door, escaped into the courtyard, and paused to collect herself as the door slammed behind her.

'I had a purpose. Oh, yes. A good scrubbing.'

The baths, public or private, seductively beckoned. Her skin itched with travel grime.

Dressmaker

Elle sur Phillary
Clothier Lilliana
Terrináe, Caetera
23 de Lares, c.3683

ELLE FELT ODDLY LIGHT in her slippers as she exited the gates of Benefactor Villaggio and took a right per Gregor's direction. Being clean helped. Rows of storefront vendors lined both sides of the narrow and cobbled street. Some had open windows, serving customers, and others had open doors with clientele streaming in and out. In the crowd, she seemed to blend in. That was a refreshingly familiar feeling, even if the dress trended toward that of a Renaissance festival.

Above the shops were windows, signaling rooms on the second floor. Most were open, and curtains billowed from some. At the third building, above the open door hung a small white-washed wooden sign with words in burned script: *Clothier Lilliana.*

Elle stepped inside. The dressmaker's shop was a circus of disorder. Forced to turn sideways, she squeezed through the bolts of material. She laughed uncomfortably at the scene once she was fully able to stand in the shop's front room. A chaotic array of scraps of material, remnants, thread, and various other sewing notions blanketed every surface. Dress forms in the corners wore partially completed attire. Clothing bags hung from rails along the ceiling, draped partially over windows, and obscured much of the light that would otherwise fill the room.

'Whoever could work in this mess?'

There was a rustling behind the counter and Elle leaned over. A wisp of a young woman was crouched and rummaging through a bin of buttons.

"Excuse me. Lilliana?" asked Elle.

The girl jumped, and the buttons rolled and bounced across the floor. The scarf tied around the mousy brown head came loose as her head hung forward in clear exasperation. When she stood, her eyes were closed. Releasing her shoulders, she opened her eyes greet Elle. "No, I'm Gianna, Lilliana's apprentice."

"May I help you with those?"

"No, no, no." She shook her head. "I'll get them later. What can I hel—"

Her mouth hung on the *l* for a moment, then she came racing around the counter and seized Elle by both arms. Elle stood straight, leaning away slightly. What the hell was this woman doing? Who greeted a stranger this way?

"You're Master Phillary's new charge! Elle, right?"

"Um...yes." Elle was still frozen, unsure how to respond to such an enthusiastic welcome and afraid she was about to wrap her in a hug. Maybe she should have gone to find Yster and brought her along to ease her introduction to this. Or, better yet, to calm this girl's reaction.

"Come...come." Words spewed as Gianna pulled Elle through the counters and into the back room. "—been expecting you—waiting for you really—we were all so pleased—wish you could have stayed for the reception—it's been five days—you're still in the entrant clothes—poor thing—where have you been? —here—have a seat." She cleared some fabric and sat Elle down, almost forcibly onto the stool and placed her hands on her hips. "Now, where is it?"

Elle's eyes stretched wide and followed the girl as she scurried around, climbing one ladder, bending low, then repeating the process, searching the shelves stacked to the ceiling. Elle opened her mouth to try to calm her commotion, but Gianna was on to something else before words could be voiced. She pulled one bundle then another from the shelves, shaking her head and tossing them on the long table. Elle held up her hands as if she could catch her in mid flutter. At least there was more room to maneuver in the back workroom.

Finally, Elle pushed out a word. "Gianna..." No reply. She raised the volume a bit. "Gianna?" Still no response. "Gianna! Can we slow down a bit?"

"Oh, here they are." Gianna pulled out a tied brown bundle from high on one of the shelves. "We guessed at your size but thought you would need something to get you started. You know that Evaluation Máda is tomorrow, right? Lilliana has been in such a tizzy—"

"Gi...a...nna..." Elle's voice grew louder.

Finally, the girl landed in one place. She placed the bundle on the table and started loosening the ties.

"Is Lilliana here? I'm supposed to give her this note."

"Oh, she'll be back soon. Making a delivery. Let's try these on. We haven't ever had the cause to pull out the brandywine shade for a female entrant. It's so exciting that Sir Phillary chose this time!"

"To be sure," Elle offered in mock agreement. She was concerned that Gianna may not get enough oxygen to her brain and pass out in mid-commotion. In fact, the young woman made Elle feel as if she had to stop for breath on her behalf.

Gianna held up a pair of wide legged pants in the brandywine. With a quick jerk, she tossed them to Elle. Then she pulled out a fitted tunic in the beige. "The tone is called fawn. These colors are so delicious. Go on...try them."

She scooted Elle toward a screen in the back of the long room. As she changed, more rustling came from outside the barrier. When Elle emerged, Gianna's eyes stretched wide, her mouth formed an O, and she clasped her hands beneath her chin.

"Just throw that grey dress into the bin over there and have a seat again. When you have time, bring back the others, too. You'll not want to wear those any more. I put your new shoes by the stool."

Elle replaced the grey slippers with ones in the same brandywine as the pants. They had done a fair job sizing as the clothes fit and bent with Elle's body nicely. Much better than the entrant-greys fit. "Was it not your shop who made the entrant clothes for me?"

"Oh, we made those too, but they're not custom. We just make those in all sizes. They just find the best fit from the stock at the bath house on campus when the entrants are prepared for the first time."

The flippancy in the description gave Elle the notion that an entrant was more like a turkey being prepared for Thanksgiving dinner than a person.

Elle was scratching her head as she put a new piece into her imaginary jigsaw puzzle when the door slammed open at the rear of the long workshop. In rushed a stack of fabric bolts on legs. When the bolts spilled onto the table, a woman who could only be Lilliana was revealed. Blonde curls stood in all directions from a slim dark face with haunting green eyes.

It was but a split second before Elle understood where Gianna had inherited her busybody manner. When Lilliana turned from the bolts on the table and looked at Elle, recognition enlarged her facial features. Before Elle knew it, someone else was rushing in her direction—hair bobbing with each step. Where Gianna halted at grasping the arms, Lilliana threw her arms around Elle with exuberance.

'Holy shit, where is Yster when I need her?'

Gathering her wits, Elle grasped this woman, holding steady and pushing her to arm's length. "Lilliana?"

"I'm sorry. I get carried away. Yes, I'm Lilliana. You're Elle. The anticipation has me feeling that I already know you." She stepped back and looked Elle up and down in the new clothes. "They are perfect for you. Did Gianna give you the cloak? It's the same brandywine shade."

"No."

Before Elle knew it, she had one of the short cloaks wrapped around her shoulders. Drawing her brows together, she looked at the absence of cover for the forearms. "Why do none of the clothes cover the arms fully?"

"Oh...that's for Flare." Lilliana waved both hands in the air like a matador dramatically teasing both bull and spectator.

'Duh...Elle.' Of course it was for Flare. Why else?

"Come here, let's take a peeksy." Lilliana grasped Elle's hands and pulled her to one side of the room, then threw a brown drape back to reveal a full-length mirror. "You're splendid in these colors—striking—fabulous—magnificent!"

Elle couldn't argue. The blacks and blues that she'd so favored back on Earth didn't compare. Bureaucracy-enforcing and a power statement were how those could best be described. This look—while simple in form—made Elle *feel* all those things Lilliana said and more. The emphasis on her natural shape—rather than straight lines of business suits—and the feel of the cloth against her skin made her feel...uh...well...that frilly, fairytale, Disney-ish word she'd always avoided.

Pretty.

"Here," Lilliana called her away from her flushed reflection. She pulled a bolt of fabric from yet another stash, and with a jerk, fanned the shimmering burgundy fabric over the table. Then another tug sprayed a fawn fabric with a similar sheen across the brandywine.

"Let's measure! Gianna!"

Elle wondered how one could sound so utterly electrified about measuring. Hands were suddenly at her back, and she jerked her head around to Gianna who was urging the brandywine cloak from her shoulders. Elle's reproach seemed to have little effect on the dressmaker's assistant. As the cloak came free, Gianna draped it over the stool and retrieved a notebook.

Lilliana flitted around with a tape, then material, then some gadgets Elle couldn't identify, calling out numbers and vague comments about length all the while. She spun Elle, assessing. Gianna dodged and obsessively followed her mistress's every move, scrawling notes as she went. Liliana held one of Elle's arms above her head, then the other, then had Gianna pull both arms forward while she surveyed Elle from behind.

"Bellissima!" Lilliana exclaimed, throwing up her arms and tossing the tape and remnants of fabric in the air like confetti.

"Lilliana!" Elle said with a bit of force and held up the paper. "I have a bank note from Gregor for you." It didn't work. How did she get these people to listen? Elle was quickly approaching the limit of her chaos tolerance.

"You have the measures? Yes, yes. We'll get to that. You have three outfits for school and your cloak in the bundle. Gianna, pack it back up for her. What else do you need?" Her focus fluttered between the two of them so rapidly, it all came out as one rush. Gianna and Elle were left to decipher which part was addressed to whom.

Assuming the final question to be hers, Elle's answer was flat, "Formal and riding clothes."

"Ahhhh...yes. I should have considered no less for the caval-master's charge. Very well." She scampered into the front room and returned, clownish hair bouncing as she dumped some black pants in Elle's arms and handed over a pair of black boots. "The brandywine slippers fit, right?"

Elle nodded with raised brows.

"Then these boots should be fine. I will have your custom riding clothes ready in two iméri. Formal wear will take ten." She hugged Elle again across the armload. "So very happy to have you here. You may leave. Gianna...help her home. I have work." She clapped her hands twice and whirled away.

"The note?" Elle called again to her backside.

"Leave it on the table." She flicked one hand in the air and danced away to a tune Elle couldn't hear, blonde curls bobbing. Elle dropped the note and shook her head as she left the store as quickly as possible.

The return walk to Phillary House began with Gianna rambling incessantly. Feeling trounced by the flurry of activity at the shop, Elle tuned her out and picked up the pace, hoping that she would become breathless and cease the chatter. She would have loved to have asked questions, but she couldn't squeeze a word in edgewise. Elle hoped—there was that word again—that everyone here was not so giddy to meet her.

When they reached the gate, Elle opened it and turned to Gianna. "Load me up." Elle's only thought was to get away from the chaos that *was* both the dressmaker and her apprentice.

Inside, Gregor leaned against the wall to the stables.

"Bye, Elle—so nice to meet you—see you in two iméri," Gianna chanted, "—we can—"

"Bye, Gianna." Elle kicked the gate closed.

Sniggering, Gregor sauntered over and latched the gate. Continuing the chuckle, he relieved Elle's load. As his mirth grew, so did her irritation.

"You." Her voice lowered into an accusatory growl and her face grew warm with outrage. "You sent me into that insanity knowing full well what I was walking into."

"Oh..." He raised both brows. "If you really want to be entertained someday, take Niccolai in there."

Evaluation Iméra

Elle sur Phillary
Phillary House
Terrináe, Caetera
1 de Vaenar, c.3683

BREAKFAST WAS SERVED INSIDE Phillary House's kitchen at a small dinette. Rain whispered against the window and blurred the garden scene to the rear of the house. The storm was soft, no wind or torrents to speak of, but thunder had rumbled low across the skies since the early hours. Though the watery gray dawn suited Elle's state of mind, Sirena said it would lift by mid-morning and Caetera's star would shine for the afternoon evaluation.

Gregor's Keeper insisted that Elle eat before Yster arrived in the carriage for the journey to Accademia de Terrináe, but Elle's stomach rebelled against the notion. She pushed the food around the plate. Maybe it would appear that she had eaten.

"Quit that and eat," Sirena admonished. "You can't fool me that way. You're too skinny, and you need the nutrition for today—so eat." She wiped her hands on her apron and moved to tend the dishes, shooting a glance at Elle from time to time.

More amused than chagrined by Sirena's overprotective scolding, Elle tucked her chin and stifled a smile. She did, however, obediently, pull the fork to her mouth. The concoction of meat and vegetables was rich with herbs that reminded Elle of autumn. The woman was truly a magician in the kitchen, and the combination of the rain and comfort food warmed Elle inside, soothing any anxiety brewing over the upcoming evaluation.

"Elle," Gregor's staccato tenor beckoned from the front of the house. It was time to leave.

Elle popped up from the table, her breakfast only half eaten, and moved quickly toward his voice. At the end of the hall, he stood with the front door open.

Yster waited on the step looking nervously at Gregor, but a grin spread across her face when she noticed Elle. She wore a verdant green cloak that flattered her mahogany coloring as Elle imagined spring leaves flattered a winter-barren tree.

Elle struggled to smile as she slid into her brandywine cloak and flipped the hood. She wore the riding pants and boots because of the rain, but Sirena had packed a small bag with her wide legged pants and slippers in case she had need of them. Grabbing the bag, Elle went to the door.

Yster said, “The color suits you. Ready?”

“Yes.”

Gregor held the door, and their eyes met his in passing. He projected: *'See you at gloaming.'*

Something about the eye contact combined with his tenor brushing against Elle’s mind made mental projection easier to accept. Maybe she was becoming accustomed to it. Or maybe it was just more anticipated. Elle nodded and left.

The carriage waited just outside the gates. The door was painted from top to bottom with a long vine, green leaves curling upward from the stems. The artistry stood out so much that Elle was disappointed not to feel the actual foliage when she brushed her fingertips over the image. Yster entered first. There were three others in the same deep green waiting in the carriage—two men sitting shoulder-to-shoulder obscuring someone in the back. Elle turned a confused gaze to her mentor.

"Elle, this is Avery, Max, and I think you know Nancy." Yster looked around Avery to get Nancy's attention.

Avery and Max both smiled congenially, and Nancy poked her bright blonde head around. "Elle! Nancy is so happy to see you! Where have you been?"

As she passed, Elle locked eyes with both men in silent acknowledgement. It seemed that they had grown accustomed to her third-person childlike quirk. She took the empty seat next to her fellow entrant.

"Hi, Nancy. We went to a vineyard." Elle left her answer vague, uncertain of what Nancy knew so far and recalling that she didn't like new places.

"Oh my!" She wrung her hands. "Vineyard? What is that like? The thought gives Nancy...you know...butterflies." Her eyes flitted between Elle's face and elsewhere with her speech.

"The trip was a whirlwind, but I met some really interesting people." The carriage lurched forward, catching Elle off guard. She slid backward in the seat. When she'd regained balance, she asked, "What about you?"

"Well, Nancy got all settled into Master Javine's house." Her forehead folded, then relaxed as she added, "All the Javine entrants made it okay."

All? "Nancy, exactly how many Javine entrants are there?"

"Ah." She looked at the carriage roof for a second, then back to Elle. She pointed to the two in the seat ahead. "Well, Max and Avery, of course."

Then, she stopped and tilted her head. She didn't look away from Elle, but her eyes shifted quickly like she was searching for something internally. Elle leaned toward her, hanging on her next words. Until this, she hadn't considered how many wards each benefactor would select. Gregor had never chosen, but what about the others?

Nancy bounced in her seat—a small move—seeming to prepare for her next words. She pointed as she counted off a roll-call of nine names as if she were counting around a circle at kindergarten. The names really meant nothing, but *ten* first years for *one* benefactor? Damn.

When she finished, Nancy asked, "Besides entrants, did you want to know who else lives in Javine house?"

"That'd be great!" said Elle with as much enthusiasm as she could muster, but her mind wandered. In their entrant group, only five had stayed. How many waves of entrants were there?

"Well, of course there's Yster. She's not an entrant of course. Nancy isn't sure why she still lives with Master Javine." Nancy's stark blonde brows dropped over dark eyes, expressing a puzzle that Elle shared.

Yster turned and smiled over her shoulder sweetly. "It was not long ago, Nancy, that I was an entrant. Once I've seen Elle through her first cycle, I'll move away from Javine House and into the mentors' quarters in Sud Residenze."

Nancy's head bobbled, then went into exaggeratedly long movements. "Oh, I get it!" But as quickly as her understanding arrived, it was replaced with her happy mask and she continued as if Yster had not jumped into the conversation. "Then there are his Keepers, Patrick and Erica." Her head bounced one final time at the end, and a pleased grin landed on her lips.

"Wow," Elle muttered considering the count of thirteen people in addition to this Javine character. Was Phillary House tiny in comparison? "How big is the house?"

"Oh—my—geeeeez. It's huge!" Nancy's coal colored eyes grew round, and she started to fidget with the hem of her cloak. "Nancy was terrified after Induction."

With hurried words, Elle said, "It's okay. Let's think about people instead." She took Nancy's hand hoping to stave off the rise of anxiety forming behind her eyes and words. Strange; Elle's chest constricted, but then, she could almost feel the distress flowing away and releasing its hold.

In the next instant, Nancy's entire being shifted—head, face, body. The switch was so jarring, yet so Nancy. With a slight jounce, she was facing Elle and clasped both her hands. Before Elle knew it, Nancy recapped her own experience at Clothier Lilliana, and somehow under the shared experience, Elle felt giddy along with her.

When the carriage pulled into the circle drive near the bathhouse at Accademia de Terrináe, Yster exited first and the rest followed. As Elle stepped down, she considered how peculiar it was that Nancy had shown no trace of anxiety as she relived being inside the Clothier's workshop for the first time.

Entrants Gather

Elle sur Phillary
Accademia de Terrináe
Terrináe, Caetera
1 de Vaenar, c.3683

THE SCHOOL SEEMED TO be a ghost town when they arrived. There were no others in the drive, the fields were empty, and the building was quiet. They now sat in the back row in an auditorium. One of Elle's heels bounced, increasing steadily in tempo, until she finally asked, "Why are we the only ones here?"

Yster flushed, then responded, "Master Javine overemphasizes punctuality. If you're not twenty minutes early, you're late. Everyone else should be—"

The door opened before she finished the thought, and people start filing in. When Nancy's mentor arrived, she left her chair in the back row. Elle searched a sea of unfamiliar faces for Sonia and Braeden. The room was about half full of chattering strangers when Sonia arrived. Elle raised her hand and leaned forward. Sonia returned the wave with a small shrug on her way to the front. Elle slumped in her chair, realizing that she wouldn't be able to chat with her friend.

The din of individual conversations echoed throughout the room as Elle continued her search. Relief bubbled in her chest as Braeden and Aidan entered—some of the last to arrive. They were both smashing in midnight blue pants and coffee colored tunics that accentuated their broad shoulders. Braeden had his matching cloak slung over one shoulder as he slid into the back row toward Elle.

"Is this seat taken?" he asked, shooting her a winning smile that said he was equally as happy to see her again.

The familiarity Elle felt as he asked brightened her entire day. "All yours." This man had an ease about him that was unlike any other person she had known. Breath simply came easier with him there, and Elle sat straighter crossing her legs. She just wished Sonia was there with them instead of next to the crone up front. Elle nodded toward her.

Braden followed the nod, then turned back to Elle. "Yeah. Feel sorry for Sonia with that one. We're supposed to sit with our mentors in the beginning." He shrugged and pointed with a thumb over his shoulder to Aidan who peered around Braeden and shot her a small wave. He smiled broadly showing his pearly whites in contrast with his darkened skin.

"You lucked out with him," Elle whispered. "He seems so easygoing."

"No kidding." Braeden's brows rose. "Yster's not bad, true?"

"Nah." Elle lowered her voice and added, "Quite the little mother hen, though."

"So, Induction. You played quite the disappearing act. What gives? Where have you been? Sonia and I have been dying to know."

Elle sighed, flitting her eyes up then back to his mismatched stare. "Where do I begin? It's an incredibly long story for such a short time. Gregor took me to the plains." Elle didn't find any recognition in his face. "Oh...man. We are going to have to catch up after this testing business."

"Ya don't say?" He flashed a crooked smile.

'How,' she wondered, *'did he feel so much like home?'*

Elle's honed edge of singular focus to reunite with friends dulled, and her brain shifted into a new gear. What had happened here while she was gone? A jumble of questions warred with each other to escape. "Who's your benefactor?" Before he could answer, she added, "And who's Sonia's? And—" She bit her lip to let him reply.

He laughed. "Calm down. There's time. Aidan and I both belong to Gustava House."

"Braeden sur Gustava." Elle rolled the words around on her tongue—unable to put a face to the name.

"Yep. Degna's the benefactor. You remember...the one woman with black hair who started the banter back at Induction?"

"Ahhh... I do."

"She's—um—what you might call *dramatic*." He chuckled and shook his head. "Anyway, Sonia's is Diego Michelli. Doubt you'd recognize him since you went MIA."

Footsteps—heavy in the heel—traipsed across the classroom stage capturing the audience's collective attention front and center. The woman's blonde hair was perfectly parted to one side and cropped into a blunt sophisticated bob. Her shoes were obscured by brown wide-legged pants. A cream-colored top served as a base layer to the brown scarf draped around her neck. Embroidery along the lapel area put Elle in the mind of a graduate's trim. She carried a staff, taller than she, ornamented with a carved owl in preparation for flight.

The conversation around the room died away. Elle's humor vanished as she leaned back toward Braeden and whispered, "Nervous about this?"

"Nah...not really," he uttered, taking it in stride. That was precisely the kind of reassurance Elle craved, but her stomach was tied in knots over this evaluation business.

Gregor had been so overly reserved so far, using this as his excuse. She hoped that once this was out of the way, he'd just open up to her. Of course, he'd also hinted that he thought he knew what her Flare was. This was also necessary so that they could discuss that in the open.

The blonde woman's staff crashed to the floor—one...two...three...times calling the room of sixty-or-so gathered to a hush. Recognition dawned for Elle with the innate command of her first words.

"Entrants," she addressed the audience in the same severe tone which silenced the benefactor table at Induction. "Welcome to your evaluation. For those who don't know me yet, I am Camellia Middlemist, headmistress of Accademia de Terrináe and Benefactor of Middlemist House."

Applause erupted from a corner of the room where several entrants sat in the front row. Elle counted four unfamiliar heads and shoulders wearing the same colors as the headmistress. Her stern façade shifted toward pride, then back to business as she lifted a hand to silence the members of her House.

She continued, "I am sure there is curiosity about the coming máda, but you can rest assured that there is no need for worry. The purpose is simple: to learn about you. This will aid you, your mentor, your benefactor, and the school in preparing the best education possible."

Nudging Braeden, Elle pointed to the front where Sonia raised her hand in the second row. They shared a smile. The eagerness for learning was so very Sonia.

"Yes?" Headmistress Middlemist responded to the raised hand, professionally, but with a slight tinge of agitation at being interrupted. She obviously liked the sound of her own voice.

"How will this testing be conducted?" Sonia asked.

"You get ahead of me," the headmistress dismissed and strolled to the other side of the stage, then faced the room again. Elle admired the move—a classic one to draw and maintain the audience attention.

Camilla Middlemist continued, "There are four sections. Three are in group settings. The fourth is one-on-one. Your fellow entrants are your assigned groups. Each entrant group will receive their schedules for the máda after this introduction. Benefactors..."

Headmistress Middlemist pointed the owl on her staff above the audience's heads. Two women—including Degna—stood with four men overlooking the classroom. Eight. There were eight benefactors in total. Elle hadn't realized this was a question until she made the calculations. Induction had been too much of a blur to count. Here and now, settling in, she could. But she also wondered why Gregor wasn't here with the other seven.

Slowly, she scanned the room. She had no way to discern mentor from mentee. If half are entrants, that meant half a dozen to each benefactor! No wonder they had given Gregor such a difficult time at Induction for not sharing in the burden.

"Conferences will be held in the evening to review the results. Get your schedules in the hall." With that, she exited through a side door.

"Yster." Elle pulled her mentor closer. "How many here are mentors?"

"Oh, half," she replied. "We only handle one per season."

"Season?" asked Elle.

Yster smiled and placed a hand on Elle's arm. Easiness flowed. "The time when we bring entrants from other planes is called Entrant Season."

Numbly, Elle asked, "Do all mentors live in one of the Houses in Benefactor Villaggio?"

"No, no, but I have yet to satisfy my obligation to Master Javine." She grabbed Elle's hand and stood. "Let's get your schedule."

Elle stood but released her hand. She wanted to be in control of her own emotion. As she turned to follow the others, Braeden glanced back as if he might lose her again and gave her a small *come-on, keep-up* wave.

Testing Begins

Evaluation Iméra 1

Elle sur Phillary
Accademia de Terrináe
Terrináe, Caetera
1 de Vaenar, c.3683

YSTER SQUEEZED THROUGH THE crowd in the hall and handed Elle a schedule which contained a simple list: Physical, Chemical, Biological, Psychological. Physical first... Elle could manage that. Now that her body had recovered from the days on cavalback, she was ready to get back into an exercise routine. After all, she had to learn how to dismount from Haize with a little more ease.

"Yeah!" Braeden bumped fists with Aidan. "I totally have the first one. You ready, Elle?"

"Sure. No problem." Elle smiled at him.

Sonia sidled up to them, grabbing Elle's attention with a touch on the shoulder. "Hey, Elle. How are you?" A soft, slight crack to her voice betrayed her nerves.

"I'm great," Elle replied, then gave her a soft, hopefully, calming look. "Are you worried about the physical evaluation?"

"How'd you guess?" She chuckled nervously, her eyes darting around the gathered group. "I totally know I'm Bio. There's no point in this testing for me."

"Alright." The man's voice boomed, again shifting Elle's attention. "Physical test. Hit the baths for appropriate clothes and meet me at the course." He turned on a heel, combat-style boots, and tan cargo pants beating a quick path toward the fields. The crowd parted as he passed. He seemed familiar from Induction, and something about his features—perhaps the jawline—grated at an elusive memory from before Caetera. Elle's forehead wrinkled as she watched him march away.

"Come on," Yster said. "This test is pretty short, but you go one by one, and you'll want time to bathe before we head back to the Villaggio."

"Who is that?" Elle asked before following.

“That is Master Andreas Javine, my benefactor.” She neither smiled nor frowned, her answer matter-of-fact, betraying no details. Elle sighed, rolled her eyes, and followed along like a good little puppy.

In the baths, Yster handed her a pile of clothing like Javine’s, gave her direction to the obstacle course, and headed for the door. “I’ll see you after,” she said, then disappeared.

Elle held up and inspected the clunky cargo-style pants with disgust. She was happy that she didn’t have to stock those clothes in her wardrobe. They were downright hideous. In truth, it was hard to picture Lilliana in all her flamboyance designing something so military. The juxtaposition made her chuckle as she fastened the rough garment and tied the boots. At least those were comfortable—clunky and heavy, but comfortable nonetheless.

Walking in silence with Sonia and Nancy, Elle followed Yster’s directions to the course. Before she knew it, Braeden and Quinn stood beside them forming a line in the front of oversized parallel bars. Andreas Javine rested a hand on the bars at his shoulder height. Four unfamiliar faces led by Nicco walked up the hill and joined him. Elle rolled her eyes.

'Fabulous, he would have to be involved in this, too.'

Turning away from him, she chewed a nail and studied the bars. There must have been at least three feet between the two, and if she had to guess, they ran maybe twenty in length.

Javine boomed, "Here's how this goes. You have twelve minutes to complete this course. You start there." He pointed to the entry of the parallel bars. "I don't care how you get across the bars, but your feet can't touch the ground. This one's a gimme." His smile was raving mad.

He tilted his head for them to follow and jogged past the parallel bars. Nicco and the others followed, then the entrants. At a series of rings laid out on the ground, Javine barked, "Nicco, demonstrate. One foot in each ring all the way through. Miss one—you fail. Trip—you fail."

Elle's mouth hung open as Nicco high-kneed it through the rings. She blinked attempting to bring his legs into focus as they blurred through the obstacle.

Moving on and pointing as he went, Javine continued, "Low wall, high wall. Over, not around."

The next one was long, and as he jogged past, he instructed, "You crawl through the sand under the ropes all the way to the end."

They didn't stop for questions or demonstration again until they came to a net of rope that stretched about fifteen feet high. Braeden bounced on the balls of his feet as the group slowed down for this one. Nancy circled the rope netting, studying the obstacle. Sonia, Quinn, and Elle took the opportunity to stop the run. This one stirred some doubt. Less confident in her upper arm strength, it was quite possible the ropes would be the end of her physical test.

Javine moved on. "Whatever you do on this one, do not twist your hands or legs into the rope. Better to fall than lose a limb."

Nicco demonstrated the mentioned taboo-move, then they were off again in quick time—at least Elle thought that's what they called it in the old military movies. They passed several other obstacles, and Javine shouted instruction, but she'd tuned out, deciding that this was certainly not going to be her Flare. As she'd told Braeden before, she wasn't an athlete. Running was simple; this was not.

The leader stopped one more time and Javine lovingly said, "This is *The Weaver*," and smirked maniacally. Completing the perimeter of the circuit, they returned to the parallel bars.

"One of these gentlemen—" He gestured toward them. "—will lead you through the course, referee, and see to anyone who is injured. Remember, you fall on any, you fail. Questions?" Their pseudo-drill sergeant proclaimed more than asked.

Silence.

"Who's first?" he barked.

Elle hid a grin behind a hand as Braeden jumped at the chance. Within seconds, he was up on the parallels, one hand on each bar walking forward. He hits the ground at a dead run and attacked the rings with agile grace.

There was no waiting for one to finish before the next in line started. Nancy tackled the bars. Sonia whooped, and Elle grinned, kind of proud of Nancy's energy.

Nicco stepped forward as Elle's turn came. She tried to ignore him and shifted in her stance. It was time to focus.

She stepped to the bars and tested the distance to see if she could hand-walk across like Braeden, but quickly learned that it wouldn't be possible. Latching onto one of the bars, she threw her feet over the top and inch-wormed herself across to the other side. No one had said she was required to use both bars.

Next up was footwork. That wasn't too bad, and she was through it pretty quick.

Her referee silently watched, and as she completed the ring challenge, Nicco moved on to the next and yelled back, "Get a running start."

Elle picked up her pace and jumped as she reached the wall, hands landing on the top.

'Yes!'

She swung her legs over and hopped down to the ground, surprised at her own ability.

At the high wall, there was a rope for assistance, so she grabbed on, found some footing, and began to climb. About half way up, her arms started shaking, and her palms burned from the rope. She pressed through. Again, to her astonishment, she made it to the top. Climbing about half-way down on the other side, she released the rope and landed in a crouch. Using the momentum in her coiled muscles, she sprang back into a run for the next obstacle.

She fell to the ground and crawled through the sand under the ropes. Barring the sand in the mouth, that one was easy. Being short had some advantages. She popped out the other side and hopped to her feet.

Onward. Over one set of tied logs—not too bad—and she came to the fifteen-foot rope net. Elle inhaled and exhaled deeply a couple of times, then grabbed on with both hands. Looking down, she found a place for each of her feet and began to climb. A rhythm of right hand, left hand, right foot, left foot developed with focus. She had to search for the specific placement of each limb as she went.

'Breathe, Elle. Focus. One at a time.'

She looked up and estimated the bar to be about six feet more. She reached with her right hand and grabbed the next hold of rough rope. Her arms trembled, and legs shook. She let go with the left hand and swung it forward. Her fingertips grazed the rough fiber as they missed and slipped back to where she had gripped before. She still had hold.

'You got this, Elle.'

She closed her eyes, feeling the tempo of her heart increasing. Forcing them back open, she focused on the next placement. With a deep breath, she swung the hand up once again. That time...it missed entirely, and her right hand slipped. The bar above diminished as she fell away. All she saw before her was the blue of the sky with two moons watching as she careened toward the ground.

She landed, not in the sand, but in Nicco's arms. Elle closed her eyes and dropped her chin to her chest, taking long relieving breaths, thankful for the soft impact, but realizing the failure and growing uncomfortable in Nicco's cradle. Their eyes met. He quickly looked away and placed her on her feet, then marched back toward the beginning of the course.

"Damn." Elle stomped and balled her fists. Better than she expected, but not good enough. A growl of a sound rumbled from her chest and into her throat. Bending over, she gulped for air.

After a short fit and catching her breath, Elle trotted back to the beginning of the course. "What now?" she asked Javine.

"You're done here. Clean up." He motioned to the bath house. He made notes in a file as Elle turned to head back.

"Elle."

She pivoted toward his voice.

"I want you to join us for dinner sometime. Talk to Yster." He didn't even look up from his writing as he addressed her.

Elle took two steps toward him, "Wh—"

"Busy now. Go," he snapped.

'What's with these benefactors?' Elle wondered, trotting away. *'Why are they so approachable one minute and mercurial the next?'* She went, but when she glanced back, Javine watched her with a downright predatory grin.

Chemical Flare

Evaluation Iméra 2

Elle sur Phillary
Accademia de Terrináe
Terrináe, Caetera
2 de Vaenar, c.3683

ELLE HAD NEVER BEEN much of a cook. In Chicago, she had a restaurant at hand for every occasion If she wanted a good beer selection and classic reminiscence of Chicago's history, The Berghoff. Her go-to diner was Lou Mitchell's. Won Kow had her covered in Chinatown. And here, her meals had all been prepared either by the serving people—whoever they were—at the Accademia during her first week here or by Sirena. Gregor mentioned that her Flare was Chemical, and Elle had delighted in her warm home-cooked meals at Phillary House. Why she'd never considered a personal chef in Chicago was now a mystery.

But Elle harbored no talent for cooking. She didn't think she could even boil water.

Knowing her shortcoming in this space, she left Yster's side and entered the classroom with an odd blend of trepidation and curiosity. To her surprise, as the door slammed shut behind her, she stood in what appeared a typical school science lab. Black-top tables were lined up in two columns with another at the head of the class, presumably for the instructor. The tables toward the front of the room were covered with vials, tubes, beakers, and a number of other unfamiliar instruments. The four others in her entrant group gathered around an empty table in the rear of the room, and she joined them.

"You should have seen Nancy tackle The Weaver!" Braeden—naturally the center of attention—hugged Nancy around the shoulders. "L'il girl has agility you wouldn't believe."

Cheeks glowing, she giggled and said, "Nancy is embarrassed." Under Braeden's playful hug and release, she stumbled a bit. "It wasn't that hard. Nancy just twisted the ropes, so they held her up," she said, shrugging. "Anyway, how long did it take you? All of six minutes?"

Sonia chimed in, "Y'all were amazing. Elle, how'd you do? I saw you starting that rope thing before I was shooed away to the baths." She mimicked climbing with her hands.

Elle shrugged. "Well, I thought I was doing okay. Arms were burning tired, but I was getting through it. If that's the last you saw, you just missed my—quite literal—fall from grace."

A few moans and light chuckles resounded around the table.

"Ha. Punny!" Nancy slapped the table and smiled wide.

"You completed in time, right?" Elle asked Nancy.

"Yes...Nancy doesn't know what that means though." Her expression was typical—alight with her first thought, a pause, then scrunched up with the next.

"Well, I suppose it means your Flare is physical, right?" Elle's words spilled out as if it were so simple, then she pulled her brows together, feeling akin to Nancy's shift to confusion and realizing that she also wasn't quite sure what it really meant either.

"Not mine," Sonia said with a laugh. "I was happy to go last. Meant no one saw me fall off the parallel bars before I even got started. I coulda told 'em and saved the trouble." She rolled her eyes.

Quinn had been standing with his arms crossed and refusing to join the conversation. When he did, his voice resonated deeper than she'd envisioned. "They pulled me at the footwork. Probably a good thing too. I've broken my nose one too many times." He rubbed the bridge where it hooked.

Elle's fellow entrants followed her lead as she leaned onto the table with both arms crossed. She lowered her voice, "What do you know about this Flare thing? I'm quite frankly confused. So what if you do have a Physical Flare, or Chemical, Biological, or Psychological? What does it mean?"

A door slammed open. The five entrants jumped back from the table and faced the door as if they were caught in the midst of some big conspiracy. A short, balding man shuffled in, carrying a flaming chalice in one hand a tray full of instruments in the other. The door swung slowly shut behind him.

Without introduction, he started, in a heavily accented voice. "Peeck table." His voice was overly loud for his tiny frame as he placed both objects on a counter at the front of the room. "One to table." He rushed around the room dropping clear eye protection on each of the tables that were already laden with experiment supplies.

Elle exchanged pensive glances with the others before the group dispersed to the tables as directed.

"I'm Dmitri Ivanov." His steps were short and dragged as he started toward the front of the room. "You call me Ivan."

Sonia's bulging eyes locked with Elle's across the aisle as he passed between them. He was likely shorter than Elle, but it was hard to be sure from a distance. That alone made him an oddity, but the accent and his tone added to the peculiarity. How was it that everyone she met in this place was eccentric in some way? Was that what she had to look forward to?

"Cheemical Flare mean you sense cheemical reaction." He waved his hands above his head as if the motion matched his words. Scurrying to the side of the room where daylight poured in, he pulled one blackening curtain after another over the windows. "We test for Flare." His words flowed up and down placing emphasis on *test* and *Flare.*

When the room was dark, save for small lines around the edges of the curtains and the flaming chalice on the instructor desk, he scuffled back to the front.

"'S seemple test. You make tornado," he said.

He placed a tray in the center of his table and rifled through the vials on the tray. "Ahh. Look a'dis...preddy awesome."

Ivan grabbed a beaker, poured in some liquid, then added something from four of the vials. Elle squinted to see if she could tell which vials he used, but the lighting was too dim, and all the vials looked alike. He swirled the liquid in a beaker, then crouching so that he looked the tray at eye level, he poured some of the liquid onto the tray.

"Nod verra much, cuz I don' wanna speel it," he said.

When satisfied, he stood and gave the tray a spin. With a long wooden stick, he grabbed a lick of flame from the chalice. Touching the makeshift match to the liquid, a green flame spurted up and began to rotate into the form of a tornado.

Elle's gasp was echoed by her fellow entrants'. Quinn leaned closer, and, of course, Nancy clapped.

"Isn'a id maybe insane how beaudiful it eez?" Ivan's question lilted. He motioned with both hands from the bottom of the green-dancing flame to where it widened forming the funnel above his head. "Look how lights up id eez!"

Before anyone could ask questions, he shifted gears and was straight to business. "Just example. Now you. One hour." He covered the spinning flame with a screen, and it ceased to dance. Elle's mouth was cotton-dry as Ivan pulled an hourglass from beneath the table and set a timer.

Quinn, at the table in front of Elle, dove into the chemicals laid out on the table. He carefully smelled each one and poured several into his palms, discarding some in a small bin at the end of his table. Before long, he started mixing several of the powders in small vials, testing the reactions. It seemed apparent where his Flare would lie.

Elle hadn't a clue what any of the crap on the table was. Test tubes and beakers were familiar, but the other pieces of apparatus were a mystery. Almost without her permission, her hand crept toward the eye-protection. In her periphery, Sonia examined the contents of the vials on the table, like Quinn. Unlike them, Elle's experience with chemistry—well, any lab science for that matter—was always exhausting and required way too much effort. Back in college, she had pulled out an A in chemistry through sheer force of will and tons of tutoring. She rolled her eyes and reached for the jars of liquid.

Smelling each one, she chose the one that nearly singed her nose hairs. It had to burn, right? She poured the liquid in a beaker then shifted to the rows of vials containing various colored powders. She read one unrecognizable label after another—Arxylicum, Brovulene, Petroxalune... If she had known any of these words at one time, she'd long since forgotten. She placed the vial in her hand back in its home, sighed, and dropped her hands to her sides.

'How am I going to figure this one out?'

Across the aisle, Sonia mixed small amounts in the empty test tubes. Thinking that a good idea, Elle found a dropper in the tool bin and put a few drops of nose-burning liquid in each of the empty tubes in the rack. There weren't *that* many combinations available, but more than she could test in the eighteen tubes she had available or the time she had remaining. She only needed to get one to light green, right?

Trial and error, it is.

There were paper and pencil to keep notes, so she began.

She put various combinations of four chemicals in each of the tubes in tiny quantities. As she dropped them in, she stood as far back as possible in an attempt to avoid injury from any reactions that didn't even need the flame. There was some kind of pure insanity to the ignorance of that exercise, but she persevered.

Elle stopped mixing the tiny solutions and watched when Quinn approached the instructor's desk. She wasn't alone in watching as he poured his liquid and lit a stick. The silence was deafening as the flame progressed in slow motion from the chalice to the spinning tray. When it made contact, a small burst of blue flame flashed. Along with her fellow entrants, Elle gasped. When it died, they groaned. Then, without further interference, a green flame grew, danced, and revolved into a similar funnel to Ivan's.

"Eeeee," Nancy squealed and clapped. Elle found herself clapping along at his success.

"Verra good," Ivan said to Quinn, then to the rest of the room, "Preddy amazing, huh?" Ivan smothered the green tornado, smiled, and held a hand toward the door for Quinn to exit. As the hook-nosed entrant loafed toward the door, Ivan made notes on his clipboard.

The door whispered shut, enclosing the four remaining entrants to complete the task. Ivan cleaned up after Quinn to allow for the next attempt. At the corner of the instructor's table, the hourglass had only spilled a quarter of the sand into a neat little dune, but Elle had mixed a solution into the last of her empty test tubes.

She grasped onto the rack of tubes and looked at the chalice. Sucking in a deep breath, she thought, *'Here goes nothing.'* She walked to the front of the room and looked around to her peers to make sure none were ready. This could take a while, and she didn't want to stop anyone else from completing the test.

She poured the first onto the tray and grabbed a stick to light it. *'Please give off a green flame.'* She brought the burning stick to the liquid. The flame sizzled to a halt with a tiny tongue of smoke rising from the extinguished stick.

Pursing her lips, she made a small noise in her throat, cleaned up the liquid, and moved on to the next solution. With every attempt, Elle held her breath until the flame was extinguished. From the end of the table, Ivan watched—arms across his chest. By the time she had completed the twelfth test, she'd lost hope.

Moving on, she held the flame to the next solution—certain that she'd have the same petering results. It erupted in a crashing boom. All eyes jumped to the front of the room as orange and yellow flames flicked. Tiny sparks flew like sparklers from the miniscule drop. Elle squinted and recoiled from the sudden flash and strobing sparks. Smoke billowed to the ceiling.

Ivan jumped and threw the screen over the plate, and the flames ceased. The cloud of glowing yellow smoke crawled across the ceiling. Ivan glared at Elle. The smoke glowed for a few seconds more, then dissipated. Once it was gone, her shoulders hunched. Ivan held her stare, moving his head left...then right...left...right.

"Mind own business," he said to the class and pointed Elle to the door. "No Cheemical."

She wasn't really surprised by the results, but the second failed attempt sat like a rock in Elle's stomach. Outside the Chemical Flare testing room, she found Quinn sitting on the ground, arms resting on bent knees, his head and back against the wall. His eyes were closed, but they opened to greet Elle when she joined him.

Quinn wrinkled his hooked nose. "Doesn't smell right."

Elle slid down the wall and took a seat beside him. She had no clue what 'right' smelled like. Instead, referencing his attire, she asked, "Middlemist, huh?"

He laughed once and fingered the brown cloak resting beside him as if he was uncertain about his Benefactory House. "Yeah. The other Middlemist residents were quite rowdy in the meeting hall yesterday." Chagrin dripped from his words. "I assume by the explosion in there that you didn't do so well?"

"Crashed and burned." Elle was pretty sure that her attempt to laugh off discomfort was unsuccessful, but at least she tried. "How'd you do that? None of those chemical names were even familiar to me."

"You want the honest answer?" His eyes shifted sideways to Elle, but he didn't turn to face her.

"I absolutely want the honest answer." Anything less would make her crazy. She had enough to figure out about this place, and now her Flare. There was no time to spend sorting through the other stuff.

Quinn shifted his body to face Elle and looked up at the door before he spoke. "So, this will sound off the wall."

"Okay?" Elle raised her brows. "Ya know, it's not like anything about this whole place is what I'd call *run-of-the-mill.*"

"Yeah. Guess that's why I'm sharing. Though it's hard to think of the words to explain." After a long pause, he continued, "There is a certain feel to substances—really anything I touch. Some are warm...some are cold...some have an almost electrical shock. The feel usually gives me a clue as to what the reactions will be." He hesitated again. "Do you think I'm crazy yet?"

"I would have a few weeks back. Not now..." Elle shook her head. "Did you know before you came here?"

He nodded. "But it's grown stronger over the last couple of weeks—er máda, I guess I should say."

Elle chewed her lip. That explained *his* decision to stay. It was still tough to explain her own, but she was acclimating and had grown hopeful that learning about this supposed Flare would help it all make more sense.

The door opened, a new, and a rancid stench wafted into the hall. Braeden stepped through and grinned.

Interlude

Evaluation Iméra 3

Elle sur Phillary
Accademia de Terrináe
Terrináe, Caetera
3 de Vaenar, c.3683

THE SUN WAS HIGH midway through second Trivium. Elle's group had completed the test for Biological Flare, and they gathered at the fields once dismissed. Elle's peers sat on their color-coded cloaks on the slope overlooking the track and field. With Sonia having passed the Biological Flare evaluation in record time, everyone except Elle now had a good idea about his or her Flare.

Elle balled her cloak and lay back onto the incline of the grassy hill. She was still a bit light-in-the-head from the sight of the dissected animal used in the last evaluation—wapatito, she thought it was. After passing out cold, it was needless to say that her Flare was *not* Biological. That only left Psychological, but she couldn't fathom how that could be the case. Maybe, another thought crossed her mind. She would be the first in Terrinian history to *not* have a Flare. She sighed and draped an arm over her eyes to block out the sun.

"Hey...let's kick around the ball," Braeden suggested and jogged down the hill before anyone could muster a reply.

Quinn and Nancy joined him, but Sonia remained at Elle's side. A consistent crease of worry sat on her forehead.

"I'm fine if you want to go," Elle said. "Just want to rest here a bit."

"You hit the floor pretty hard back there. Someone should stay with you. Anyway, remember...physical is not my thing." Sonia reached out.

Elle's arm tensed under Sonia's light touch, and Gregor's tenor echoed back to her: *"Yster and other mentors can calm your anxiety. That's biological Flare."*

When there were no foreign sensations, she forced her muscles to relent and allowed her eyes to drift shut. "Sonia, do you understand your Flare?"

"No way! I've just always had a fascination with biology, so it makes total sense. I'm dying to get into school to learn all about it."

Elle didn't open her eyes, but she could envision Sonia's excitement about the prospect behind her lids. "I'm happy for you...and Quinn...and the others. It's just..." The thoughts couldn't get past the lump in Elle's throat. She swallowed, considering how much she left behind and the new concern that she might not really fit in here. Finally, *something* managed to squeeze out. "What if...I uh...don't have one?" The stumbling words weren't clear, but Elle hoped it was enough for her friend to follow.

"Oh, Elle." Sonia's voice took on a soothing tone. "You know, passing out can have emotional effects too. Just be patient through the rest of the evaluation. We don't really know what these results mean yet anyway."

"Yeah...okay." The logical part of her brain knew Sonia was right, but patience wasn't her forte. Elle considered voicing her concerns to her friend. Her training in communication didn't really constitute a Flare or any other special talent, and there seemed to be so little business here, in Caetera. Would they send her back if she failed all the evaluations? Maybe that was a good thing. Maybe not. Elle was more confused now than ever, so it was better she just kept quiet. In the silence that followed, Elle breathed in the floral-fresh air until she drifted off under the warmth of Caetera's star.

Psychological

Evaluation Iméra 4

Elle sur Phillary
Accademia de Terrináe
Terrináe, Caetera
4 de Vaenar, c.3683

ELLE SAT BESIDE YSTER with an eerie sense of déjà vu. For the fourth, and final iméra, they returned to the auditorium where the máda and the evaluation had begun. Clearly, Elle required testing for psychological Flare. Each of the others, however, had shown competency in one of the other Flares. Apparently, everyone had to complete all the tests, and the official results would be shared in a private conference after all sessions were complete.

The inside of Elle's lip was raw from where she'd been chewing all week, and now, she couldn't keep her leg from bouncing in the tense silence that plagued the group. With the mentors so close, the ease the entrants had developed over the last three iméra vanished. She couldn't figure out why the mentors were present. They hadn't stayed for the other tests.

Ready to be on with the last session, she leaned over to Yster and asked, "How does this one go?"

"The evaluation for psychological Flare is a set of two interviews. You will meet with voteri of the Second and Fifth Holy Unities individually."

Elle tilted her head and squinted, scrolling through her memory of the voteri from the strange ceremony shortly after her arrival. All she could recall was color. She couldn't align the second and fifth with specific memories. "Remind me which ones those are," she prompted.

"Oh." Yster patiently smiled, and explained, "The Second Holy Unity is dedicated to love—Votoro D'Alphinus and Votara D'Alphiné. They wore the dusty rose color in the blessing. The Fifth is Unity of Discord and Harmony. I think you'll recall their spectacle." Her eyes crinkled in the corners.

"Ah...yes, the sprite-like pair." Their colorful tumbling appearance had broken the severity of the ceremony. At least those two seemed to be lightly entertaining. Maybe it wouldn't be so bad, but interviews? "But how do the—"

“Elle sur Phillary,” Camellia Middlemist called from the front of the room.

Elle gripped the chair. Of course she’d be first; the others already had a good idea of their Flares from the prior three days’ testing. She scooted forward but didn’t stand. Even though she’d questioned their presence, Elle suddenly felt reluctant to leave the safety of her mentor’s side.

Yster placed a soft hand over hers. “There isn’t a reason to worry.”

...and there it was... Elle felt the release of tension with the mentor’s touch, and for a change, was grateful.

Yster continued, “When they’re done, I’ll be there to get you.” She lifted her eyes toward Benefactor Middlemist.

Elle stood, shuffling to the aisle, then walked down to the front of the lecture hall.

“Get it, Elle!” Braeden chanted—voice low but carrying as if he were shouting across a sports field. To emphasize the cheer, he threw a fist in the air. “You got this, girl.”

Gratitude for his vote of confidence warred with lingering trepidation. When Elle looked in Sonia’s direction, she offered a simple thumbs-up. Elle could only respond to both with a feeble attempt at a smile, then she put on a mask of determination, and walked forward.

Benefactor Middlemist pointed her to an exit to one side of the front area—not quite a stage. As the door closed at her back, Elle was alone in a small room free of decoration. To her left, a table and three chairs sat in the center with nothing but the empty wall on the other side.

'Great! Where's the one-way mirror?'

There was another door directly across from the one she'd entered. Elle crossed and tried the handle. Locked—it figured. Interrogation much? She sighed and flounced into the chair facing the side of the room with the doors.

The minutes that passed seemed like hours, and boredom had her picking at a hangnail. Maybe she was nervous, too. That was a strange sensation, or strange awareness. Before Caetera, nerves were something she hadn't felt in...what, a decade? She'd lived and breathed her career. Everything in her life centered around her next promotion. She'd long since forgotten the constriction that came with real anxiety, but since coming here, every experience had been like a belt tightening around her chest.

The locked door opened and in floated a votara from the blessing ceremony in the rose-gold shimmering robes she'd worn then. Her partner was on her heels, though Votoro d'Alphinus executed marked, purposeful steps in contrast to her grace. Elle sat straighter in the chair pulling her hands into her lap, still fidgeting with the hangnail.

The woman smiled warmly. The man's face was stern, betraying no thought or feeling. They were silent as they sat side-by-side. Elle found it difficult to hold their uniformly dark eyes under the scrutiny they both exuded. Even breathing took effort. She tried to focus on Votara d'Alphiné, hoping for some clue as to her next move from her softer visage. Every few moments, Elle's eyes unwittingly flited to the solemn votoro. He sat with back straight, statue-still, and watched.

'What?' The word erupted as a scream inside Elle's head. She fought to adhere to interview etiquette and allow them the first questions, but her pulse was starting to pound. What was she supposed to do? *'What do you want from me? C'mon...please...if this is an interview, just ask questions already!'* Her internal voice twisted, demanding answers.

Votara d'Alphiné nodded with a slight, satisfied smile. "Elle, may I?" She reached a hand across the table.

Ever so slowly, Elle lifted and stretched her hand to meet the votara's. She braced herself for a voice in her mind, but unlike with Gregor, Elle didn't hear anything. She peaked her brows; there was neither a mentor's calm nor the buzzing tension she felt with Nicco. But, slowly, a wash of warm tenderness flowed into her through their connection. It wasn't the release of tension as with Yster. The warmth streamed intimately through her and built in intensity. Soon, without permission, her body reacted. Elle's back arched. She threw her head back and squirmed in the chair, striving to relieve a building tension that had no right to be taking hold of her, low in her stomach, then lower still.

Votara d'Alphiné smiled and promptly removed her hand from where theirs were intertwined. Elle's palm cooled in the absence of touch. With the severed connection, the sensations pulsated away, Elle's breath—having sped with the sudden need for release—returned to normal, and post orgasmic elasticity settled into her joints. Her face burned. She tucked her hands back into her lap and ducked her chin as if she could hide in the barren room.

"We're done." The baritone command in the votoro's voice was abrupt, jarring.

They stood, revealing their own hands joined. They must have been connected through the entirety of the awkward encounter. The temperature rose even further in the small room as Elle's chagrin renewed. Votora d'Alphiné tapped on the locked door, and it opened. She exited ahead of the votoro, who, before following, winked at Elle. The gesture was at odds with an otherwise stern demeanor. As he left, Elle dropped her head to the table.

Elle had scarcely recovered when into the room came an explosion of Votara d'Earys and Votoro d'Anaerys. Their dress was the same patchwork uniform from the garden alcove. They moved around the table in opposite, but concentric circles. Elle shifted her head from side to side, trying to keep up with the motion.

Her mind reeled, a long screech ripped through her brain, and though it didn't escape her throat, it took her breath with it. At some point during the silent scream, she closed her eyes to block the chaos, pressed her palms to her temples, and stood, feeling the need to rise above the absurdity. When her inner cry ran its course, she opened her eyes and gradually dropped her hands. Both patchwork-clad bodies stood before her shoulder-to-shoulder, heads tilted toward one another, and faces expressionless.

'Raggedy Ann and Andy.'

"Very nice to meet you, Elle." Votara d'Earys curtsied, opened the door, and left, though Elle could have sworn it had been locked before.

Votoro d'Aenerys beamed a long, toothy grin. Elle waited for his next move. At length, with one hand wrapped around his torso in front and the other in back, he bowed stiffly from the waist, the action reminiscent of a toy soldier in *The Nutcracker.* He said nothing and opened the door, following his other half.

Elle collapsed in the chair with her head in her hands. She swallowed repeatedly, working to dislodge the lump in her throat and desperately trying to put her mind back together after both the sexual intrusion and the forced chaos. That was it? There was nothing to have passed or to have failed, only something that felt hauntingly like she'd been mentally stripped and broken. So what came next? Four days of testing and nothing about her Flare had become clear. She felt alone—more alone than after being abandoned to foster care. Trapped between worlds, truly belonging to neither, and given no clues from the so-called evaluation process, she grew more confident that she should have chosen differently at Induction.

A knock sounded at the door.

Elle sat back and sighed, resigned. "Yeah?"

Yster poked in her head. “They’re preparing for the conference with Master Phillary. Ready?”

Cera and Gregor

Cera, Votara d'Alphiné
Accademia de Terrináe
Terrináe, Caetera
4 de Vaenar, c.3683

CERA CRIED ONTO HIS strong shoulder. The Votoro d'Alphinus, priest of the Second Holy Unity, Devan, held the priestess as she wept into his shoulder. Cera was thankful for the man she now considered her better half. Their arrangement as Votoro and Votara of a Holy Unity wasn't so much a marriage as it was an arrangement of balance. His manifestation of the precepts of Alphinus was strong and sometimes harsh, while Cera's practice in the ways of Alphiné was emotional, loving, and sometimes broken. His strength often held her together.

She could always turn to Devan, and after the evaluation of Elle sur Phillary, she needed someone to lean on. Elle's Flare was most definitely Psychological. It was strong, and it was too traumatically familiar. Cera's breasts, though long healed, ached at the feel of such a flare.

"Love," said Devan, holding her out from him a bit so he could look into her eyes. "Maybe it should be I who trains this girl. This will break you all over again."

Cera pulled from his embrace, wiping her eyes. It was time to be strong. Alphiné brought this burden before her, and she would serve her Holy Unity as the precepts required. "No, Devan, it is my charge to guide those with Psychological Flare. Alphiné and Vaena would not have seen her into our plane, and the Holy Second would not demand this of me unless I was ready."

"How can I help?" asked Devan, ever her rock.

"Be there for me when I am done with the conference. I'll need the blessing of our Holy Unity." She turned to him, having dried her eyes, and smiled.

"Always."

"Facing Gregor will be the hardest part. I fear he has never healed—neither from Renaud's torture nor from our parting."

Aftermath

Yster sur Javine
Accademia de Terrináe
Terrináe, Caetera
4 de Vaenar, c.3683

YSTER'S SMILE FADED WITH one look at Elle. The young redhead had bags under her eyes, so deep that she wondered if she'd slept the night before. She made a mental note to make a side trip to Uchi, her partner's small home, and package some of Natsue's water-blooming Suiren petals, then she'd deliver them to Phillary House before gloaming. In addition to their anti-inflammatory properties, they also calmed the senses and helped one sleep.

Elle dropped her arm from her forehead to the table and held Yster's gaze. Conscious of Elle's tenuous state of mind, Yster started for the table. Elle's chin quivered, and she looked away. Her face grew visibly heavy, drooped, and finally melted into tears. She turned in slow motion, draped an arm over the back of the chair, and slumped sideways.

The other entrants waited for the room, so Yster went to the other door and stuck her head out. Camellia Middlemist raised a perfect blonde brow at her with an obvious question. In a whisper, Yster said, "Mistress Middlemist...I am going to need a few minutes here with Elle."

Closing the door, she pulled a chair around the table to face Elle, whose eyes were closed. Yster sat with their knees touching and then by instinct and training, she started to reach for Elle but stayed her hand. Instead, she said, "Elle, I don't want to further upset you, but may I help?"

Elle held her eyes tight, then squeezed even tighter.

'Would it be so wrong to accept her offer now? Am I running from what I need to feel? That peace she offers must be addictive? Maybe? No, Elle, you can do this—on your own.'

As Elle's words swept through Yster's mind, she chewed a lip and restrained her hands in her lap.

"I think I'll be okay." Elle sighed, sniffed, and quirked the corner of her mouth.

"Very well," said Yster as she pulled a tissue from her pocket and offered it to Elle. She couldn't say—no, wasn't allowed to say—anything to reveal that Elle projected her thoughts telepathically. She struggled for a moment with what to say next. Elle obviously needed comfort, but not the kind that Yster's Flare provided. "I'm not sure I could help with this much anxiety anyway."

Elle frowned and turned her head slightly, wiping her nose. "What do you mean by that?" she asked. "It's helped my anxiety before."

"My Flare is Biological. It has limitations on how it can affect your mental state. It stimulates your body to release hormones that relieve or increase tension. However, I also need to be clear on which hormones to manipulate. I'm not clear right now, and there are natural limitations. It might exacerbate your current anxiety." Yster's training had involved many cycles of studying how her touch could trigger hormones, but they were still tricky to work with.

"Oh." Elle mustered a weak laugh.

Using what she had left for comfort, her compassion, Yster soothed, "You've been through a lot." Her voice cracked. Hoping Elle wouldn't notice, she continued in a slight rush, "It is truly okay to feel this way... It's really too much to put one person through in a single day."

"Ya think?" Elle sniffed. "After that, I'm pretty sure staying here was a mistake."

In a lapse, Yster reached forward again but stopped midway. "I think you're wrong. You belong here." She turned to rest an arm on the table. "More than you know."

Elle rolled her eyes and laughed—a singular sort of laugh. "Hate to sound like a broken record, but what exactly do you mean by *that*?"

"Elle," Yster pleaded. "Think about the connections you've made already. Nancy adores you. Braeden and Sonia. I see the four of you becoming very close friends. How much of that did you have back on Earth?"

Elle thought for a long moment, mentally silent this time. At last, her eyes widened, and she finally responded, "Observant."

"Well that *is* my job," said Yster, smiling. Elle's breathing was leveling off, and the tears had stopped. Yster didn't touch Elle's skin where her Flare would take effect but placed a hand on her knee. "Let me tell you about my evaluation," she said. Though she tried to hide any warning, it was tough. Her own evaluation had been quite traumatic as well, and as she spoke, she felt like she was giving advice to someone about to give birth.

"As an entrant," Yster began, smiling reminiscently. She hadn't told this in a long time, and while she had grown to love Terrináe with all her heart, those times were hard. "I was clueless. Where you picked up on my touch during Induction Máda, I was oblivious. My mentor was Margaret—that's Sonia's mentor."

Elle raised her brows. *'The crone?'*

Yster nodded at Elle's candid realization, then continued, "Master Javine was a new benefactor at the time, and I was his first chosen entrant. He was—and still is—distant with his entrants before the testing. I had no understanding of what the evaluation was when it started."

Elle interjected, "So, I have much to be thankful for with Gregor."

"I can't compare really. Master Javine was okay after we had our Flares identified. Still a little more rigid than the others from what I understand. Of course, there's no one who has been part of Phillary House to compare notes with." Yster cleared her throat. "Anyway, my first test was Psychological." Raising her brows, she met Elle's deep blue stare. "Can you imagine what you just went through as your first session?"

Elle shook her head. “Wow. No. I can’t.”

Yster leaned on the table and traced the wood grain with her thumbnail. “I felt almost ravaged when Votara d’Alphiné spoke in my mind.”

Elle pursed her lips and pushed them to one side. *‘That was* not *what I experienced.’*

Yster continued, stifling a reply, “...and the voteri from the fifth unity just flat-out scared me when they entered. I sat stock-still, ready to ball up in the corner.”

‘That, I could see...’ Elle sat forward, leaning onto the table.

“My second test was for the Biological Flare. I know you didn’t make it to the end, but after you walk through the dissection entirely, there is an interview about your experience. I felt insane having to describe that I saw small glowing lines moving in and out of the tissues within the dissection,” said Yster.

“I suppose those were the hormones?” asked Elle

Yster nodded again, sat back, and shrugged both shoulders. “The rest of the day was pretty uneventful—”

A quick tapping sounded at the door before it opened. “I’m sorry,” said Camellia Middlemist, but her all-business façade said otherwise. “But we need the room.”

“We’re ready, right?” Yster looked to Elle.

“Oh, yes. Sorry.” They stood and exited the small room, heading away from the auditorium and to the conference with Gregor Phillary.

It was clear that Elle was nervous to learn the truth about her Flare, but Yster’s stomach was tied in knots as well. She couldn’t quite decide if she was nervous for Elle or intimidated by the elusive Master Phillary.

Conference

Elle sur Phillary
Accademia de Terrináe
Terrináe, Caetera
4 de Vaenar, c.3683

"WE'RE READY, RIGHT?" YSTER looked inquiringly at Elle.

"Oh, yes. Sorry." Elle stood and returned her chair to its home, and they exited through the once-locked door. The one that led somewhere new, somewhere *other* than the auditorium. Uncertainty had Elle's stomach in a vice grip as they made the journey to where her benefactor awaited, down one side of a wide hall divided lengthwise by a planter full of the Noctilucent Clarets.

The entire journey was likely less than a couple hundred paces. When they reached an indistinct door and Yster reached for the handle, Elle grasped her arm before she pulled it ajar, suddenly feeling the need for intervention. She'd worried before if Yster's touch was addictive like a drug, but she no longer cared. Elle had always been told that her face was overly expressive, and Yster confirmed that rumor with a gentle smile.

"Of course." She took both Elle's hands in her own and closed her eyes.

A cool flow, releasing tension in every muscle, washed from the center of Elle's neck, down her arms, through her body, and finally down her legs. Her thoughts were still intact as they were before Yster's mentor-touch but moved slightly out of focus. The physical release of muscles merely eased her mental processes rather than erasing the thoughts altogether. "Wow, now that I understand the hormone thing, I get what you mean by it possibly not helping with certain heightened emotion...thank you for that."

"Elle, this should be exciting for you." Yster squeezed her hands.

"Gotta be honest. It feels more like I'm being put on display—bared for all to see. And to top it off, I have yet to prepare."

A remembered lunch with Ralph, one of Elle's favorite professional mentors, materialized in her mind's eye. In the vision, it's was her first corporate job. He sat across a booth table at their weekly lunch. Elle could even hear his voice—a brown sugar alto that didn't fit the very large, bald man.

'Elle, there are three rules to presenting. Always be prepared. Always present with confidence. And always believe in what you present.'

Yster dropped her brows and tilted her head slightly.

"What?" asked Elle.

Shaking her head, Yster broke contact and wiped her palms on her cloak. "It's just that...well, there's nothing for you to present, so no need for such confidence."

Elle gasped, eyes popping wide. "You heard me. My thoughts."

Yster's mouth formed an O. "No, no." She waved both hands, nervously synchronized with the shaking of her head.

Crossing her arms, Elle stared her down, daring her to keep up the pretense.

Yster closed her eyes and inhaled through her nose, her chest expanding on the long breath and her hands balling into fists. Then she composed herself enough to whisper, "Elle. Please. We need to do this conference. It is not my place to share these things with you before..." She pressed her mouth together tight, twitched her head, then continued, "Are you ready?"

Elle's stomach flopped, and she felt a bit weightless. No clue how she'd done it, or how to control it, but Yster had *heard* her. *'I do have a Flare.'* Elle's head dropped back, her eyes closed, and she exhaled her relief. Then she faced Yster, and with a growing grin, she said, "Let's go."

"Please don't let on that I, um..."

This is the first Elle had seen a fluster, and it drew her to Yster more so than when she projected her motherly charm. Light pink colored her cheeks, and she looked ten years younger. Elle winked at her. "It's our secret."

Yster pushed the door inward. In the reveal, Votara d'Alphiné and Gregor faced off on opposite sides of a square table with four chairs. There was a window on the far wall and bureau to one side, holding a planter brimming with more Clarets. There was utter silence between the two, and the floral-scented air seemed so thick that it could be sliced.

Gregor looked up when Elle entered. *'It's about time.'*

"Hello to you, too." As Elle was still a little high from her discovery in the hall, she intended the words to be in jest, but they sounded bitter.

"Hello, Elle," he said aloud, dryly.

Votara d'Alphiné gave Gregor a sideways look, then greeted the newcomers with honeyed sweetness, "Yster. Elle. Please, have a seat, and we'll get started."

Yster took the seat farthest from the door. Gregor's posture relaxed as he crossed one foot to rest on the other knee, but he carefully trained his gaze down, away from Votara d'Alphiné.

Eyeing the file that rested on the table, Elle sank into the last remaining chair. "So, how does this play out?" she asked, hoping to break the tension.

"First, Votara d'Alphiné is a mouthful. You may simply call me Cera," said the votara. "I will begin by saying that you are very fortunate that Gregor has accepted you into his household."

Strange, she gave him a compliment, but there was something that simmered between them when they made eye contact. "Why is that?" Elle prompted.

"Because he is the only benefactor whose Flare is Psychological. He is what we call a Psy-comm. He'll help you learn to use and control your own Psychological Flare."

"That makes sense, I guess." Elle narrowed her eyes, turning from Cera to Gregor, trying to discern why there was so much strain.

At first, he didn't look up from the table, but he must have felt her stare. In this room—for that matter, in Terrináe—he was cold and hard. When his eyes finally found Elle's, they belonged to the Gregor who emerged while they were at the vineyard. He was indeed the more relaxed man who taught Elle the dance by the fire. "It's the reason I selected you. You are the first entrant I ever *heard* during Induction."

Elle's hand found its way to her throat. Unable to hide her shock at his revelation, she asked, "What? What did you hear?"

He quirked an eyebrow, and his tenor was warm. "You spoke to yourself about having confidence." *'And something about a flaming path,'* he voiced only in her mind. A question about that was betrayed on his face for a split second before he returned to his all-business mode.

"There's more, though." His words and swift swivel of his head threw the focus back to Cera. Under the demand for her to continue, Cera patted her coifed black up-do, seemingly stalling.

Elle cleared her throat. "I'm sure. If that were all, I doubt there would be so much tension in this room."

"Elle, the four of us who evaluated you for Psychological Flare discussed afterward." Cera propped her elbows on the table and leaned toward Elle. "I have been doing this for near four-hundred cycles, and this is only a second for me. We have only crossed one other with a Flare that felt so...volatile."

Volatile. That was about the last description Elle wanted to hear in relation to her Flare. That made it sound somehow dangerous. "I, uh, don't understand."

Everyone in the room watched her, and she searched each of their faces in turn. Cera was pensive, Yster stoic, and Gregor insistent. Cera's eyes flitted under Gregor's silent demands. What was she hiding? He held her trapped in his gaze, though as far as Elle could tell, he was silent, both audibly and mentally.

"Cera, cut the crap," Gregor snapped after a long, tense silence. He dropped his foot to the floor and sat forward, face-to-face with Cera. He didn't take his eyes from hers when he said, "Elle, you have deeper talents than they can identify, and it scares them. Your psych eval was..." Ever-so-slightly, he tilted his head and drawled "...*unusual*." Accusation clearly intended.

Elle recoiled from the tabletop conflict.

Gregor grabbed the folder and opened it to a handwritten page. He pointed to the script, eyes still boring into Cera's, and said to her, "Explain the details you wrote to her. Make it quick."

"Very well." Her tone was equally cold but softened when she turned to Elle. "When I touched you, I sent some thoughts your way—warm thoughts of fondness and ahem...romance."

The flames in Elle's cheeks rekindled as she was reminded of that particular discomfort.

"It's hard to describe, but you pulled on my thoughts and formed them into something far more than they were intended—something raw and primal. My partner, Devan also felt the pull."

Elle's mouth hung, and her brows raised. She could *not* be hearing this correctly. "That was *me*?"

Gravely, Cera nodded. "As Gregor said, we don't fully understand it yet."

"So, what about this other person you say had a similar Flare? What happened to him?" Inside her own mind, Elle reeled. '*Incredible! You must know something! You brought me to this place! You evaluated me! You are supposed to be the experts here!*'

"I wish I had more answers for you, but we will explore and learn about it in school. And yes, I heard your outrage and questions. I'm guessing Gregor did, too." Without moving her head, she raised her brows and looked sideways at him.

When he gave one short nod, Elle shot a questioning gaze at Yster. She pursed her lips and shook her head. Whatever she'd communicated was reserved for those with Psychological Flare—maybe?

"About the other Flare, I think it's best if we focus on you for now," Cera demurred.

'I agree with her there,' Gregor projected. His cold stare softened again when he turned away from Cera to face Elle. *'I promise to share that later. This is about you right now.'*

Gregor had been true to his word so far, so Elle decided that it could wait. *'But how did I ... emotion ... yelling ... anger ... what? I don't get it.'* Elle shook her head at her own jumble of thoughts—clearly, exhaustion had taken over from the mental gymnastics. She sighed. "So, Cera, what are the next steps?"

"Well, the classes you attend will be crafted around what we know. What we don't, we'll learn as we go. Many classes will align with the other entrants' schedules. However, you'll have one-on-one classes to develop your Flare."

"One-on-one? With whom?"

"Me, to start. I have the most tenure here instructing in Psychological Flares. As I said, near four hundred cycles. Even your benefactor studied under me." She smiled sweetly, knowingly at Gregor. Plainly, more lay between the two than tension over Elle's evaluation.

"That was a very long time ago, Cera," he replied without inflection. "Are we done?"

"Not quite. If it is alright with you, Elle, I would like to do a short repeat."

'Oh hell no.' Elle shook her head. The last thing she needed was to have another orgasm in front of Gregor and Yster.

Cera stalled Elle's objection by raising a hand. "More controlled this time, I promise."

"Uh...I don't think that's a good idea." Elle looked around the table.

"We can stick with very simple emotions this time. I'll break the connection if anything is going the way it did in the evaluation." Cera extended her hand.

Elle tentatively agreed, and Yster offered a hand to calm her before it began. Thankfully, Elle clasped onto her hand and immediately felt the tension releasing as hormones ran rivers of relaxation through her muscles.

Releasing Yster's hand, she looked down at Cera's, waiting patiently on the table. The tattoo on her inner forearm—two flowers, petals forming a heart-shape at the mouth of flutes, stems intertwined—gave Elle pause.

"That is the mark of the Second Holy Unity." Pride dripped from Cera's voice.

Slowly, Elle placed a hand in hers. Across the table, Yster bit her lower lip, and her brows drew together in concern. Elle feigned a smile to let her know she was okay. Then her forced smile stretched and spread across her face. Her eyes became arcs, reflecting sudden, unnatural joy. Elle's shoulders lifted, and her whole body rose, ready to spew forth the elation that bubbled up just beneath her skin.

Just before Elle jumped from the seat and gave motion to her glee, Cera released her hand, and the tide of pure exhilaration ebbed. Elle breathed slowly and closed her eyes, shoulders inching away from her ears, and the exhaustion took over once more.

"Fascinating," Cera breathed. "On the first day of school, check in with me in the morning. Yster will bring you. I'll have your schedule." She gathered the file and stood. "Gregor, so nice to see you again."

"Cera." He didn't stand to see her leave, only said, "Elle, I brought Haize. The ride home will be good for you."

He was right. The connection—cengal—with Haize was pure and simple and would be a welcome diversion from the stress of the day. After the ups and downs, Elle yearned for a retreat. She was anxious to return to Phillary House and hopeful for a simple drink to finish off the evening before falling wholeheartedly into bed.

Unfortunately, there was no doubt that Sirena would have a royal spread for their evening meal. There was a twinge at the thought of trying to force her addled brain to absorb more Suebhian in conversation with Lyall. Then there was her favorite roommate—Nicco. She cradled her head in folded arms on the table.

'Maybe I could just sleep here?'

Evaluation Complete

Elle sur Phillary
Accademia de Terrináe
Terrináe, Caetera
4 de Vaenar, c.3683

GREGOR LEFT WITH A promise to bring Haize down from the stables. Simply placing one foot in front of the other drained what little mental focus Elle had remaining. After the last four days, being physically challenged, asked to solve an impossible science problem, passing out cold, and reaching her cerebral brink, she shut off as much thought as possible. Yster held her hand in the crook of her arm and served as a crutch as they meandered in the general direction of the baths via the sports fields. If her touch numbed Elle, it was likely for the best.

"Elle!" Braeden jogged up from the field. "You okay?"

"Yeah, good." A hitch in her voice betrayed the words. Elle dropped her hand from Yster's elbow, wiped her palms on her pants, and weakly smiled. For the second time this week, a metallic taste clenched her jaws. The horizon tilted, and her eyes fluttered shut. Everything inside revolved like the green-flame tornados from the Chemical Flare exam. Once the internal churn subsided, Elle opened her eyes to find that Braeden held her weight with a hand under each elbow. Elle's cheeks burned, and she pushed away.

"Glad I'm not Psych. Seems tough." He continued to steady Elle with large hands.

An apprehensive strength crawled from his hands through Elle's arms, kneading as it went. The vigor and worry engulfed her, and Braeden's distress over her weakness turned into her own. She jerked her eyes up to meet his. Did he know? His concern amplified the contrast between his irises, one so dark the pupil was camouflaged and the other olive-green with hints of caramel.

Hastily, Elle broke both physical and eye contact. She crossed her arms, trying to rub away the distress that followed the foreign instant fortitude. "Uh. I'm okay. Really. The last couple of tests were just exhausting."

Braeden and Yster reached for Elle at the same time.

She backed away holding up both hands. "No kid gloves, guys. 'kay? I'm good."

"You do seem instantly better." He lost the crease between his brows with a shake of his head. "Anyway, we're heading down to The Whistle tomorrow for a couple of drinks. Sonia, me, Aidan. You in?"

"Sure." She nodded. "Yeah, that'd be fun."

"Yass!" His enthusiastic bounce was infectious, and Elle smiled. "We'll stop by about sundown. Laters." He waved, skipped twice, and jogged back to join Aidan at kicking the ball around the field.

"How are you?" The mother-tendency was back. Too bad; Elle had enjoyed the break in Yster's persona.

Elle shrugged. "Feeling strong, actually."

In the fountain-yard behind the baths, the Javine carriage awaited, but Gregor and the cavali hadn't arrived. A driver sat in the front seat, and there were three inside. Nancy's shoulders rose to her ears, and she waved with a huge smile painted across her face. Elle couldn't help but to smile and return a small wave. Andreas Javine stood at the carriage door. He wore the green livery of Javine House, and his thick golden hair was water-darkened, hanging loosely from its normal club.

He strode closer with purpose yet spoke casually. "Elle, will you be riding with us?" There was nothing in tone or words to cause alarm, nevertheless, Elle tensed under his address.

"Thank you, Master Javine." Her nose wrinkled at the taste of such formality. "But not today." She strove to appear regretful in her refusal and pointed down the path to where Gregor approached riding Ashe. Haize cantered alongside, and any remorse Elle could muster was erased.

He didn't look to where Elle had pointed, just pressed on. "Did you speak with Yster about dinner as I requested?"

"Oh, no. Sorry. I've had a bit on my mind today." Elle dodged the intensity of his gaze and searched for the unique comfort that Haize brought. She was eager to ride and sorely ready to be away from so many people and expectations.

Haize, untethered, broke away from Ashe and trotted straight to Elle's side. She stood slightly behind Elle, head hovering over a shoulder, but so that Elle remained mostly between her and Javine. The warmth of a smile brought on by her cat-eyed caval after the long hours of the afternoon was, in and of itself, refreshing. Elle's hand lifted to her muzzle, and the simple pleasure of cengal was amplified.

"Hi, sweet girl," Elle cooed.

Gregor dismounted in a lithe leap, sprang to standing, and moved to Elle's side. "Andreas, nice to see you."

Javine, finally breaking his focus on Elle, held out a hand. "Likewise, Gregor. I've enjoyed getting to know your new ward."

"Really?" There was a new formality in Gregor's manner. "Learn anything interesting?"

"Well, she came close to passing Physical." Javine paused and looked at Elle, pride almost dancing in his stormy eyes. "But, in the end, I believe her Flare lies elsewhere. True?" He cocked his head toward Elle.

'Why would he be proud? Or proud of me?' Was she really expected to answer that question? Elle looked to Gregor for guidance, and said, "Ah—"

"Andreas," Gregor gently admonished. "She has had a long iméra and máda and is ready for last meal."

"Speaking of..." Again, his stare released Elle, allowing her breath to resume as he faced Gregor. "We would be honored if you would both join the Javine household for dinner. There is always room."

"That is gracious of you, but Sirena has my table already prepared for evening meal. Now, if you'll excuse us." He extended the cloth ladder slung across Haize's saddle and offered a hand to Elle.

She mouthed, *Thank you,* to Gregor, and mounted Haize.

"Another time then?" Javine asked politely.

Once Gregor was comfortably astride, Ashe lowered his head to Andreas as if to answer on Gregor's behalf. With matching mere civility, Gregor replied, "Of course." Then he nudged Ashe into motion. Haize followed, and a thrum of her joy ran through Elle's hand where it rested on her neck.

Elle wondered if Haize sensed her joy in return.

Armagnac

Elle sur Phillary
Accademia de Terrináe
Terrináe, Caetera
4 de Vaenar, c.3683

THE DARK MEAT FOWL melted on Elle's tongue and restricted any praise she wished to offer for Sirena's kitchen magic, now understood to be Chemical Flare. By the silence amongst the dining company, it seemed Elle's delight was shared by Gregor, Nicco, and Lyall. The gravy-soaked meat, savory grains, and warm brown bread was a meal better the five-star restaurants that had cluttered Elle's evenings on Earth. Sirena ate slowly, and her eyes glinted as she observed the gluttony exhibited by the members of Phillary House.

Gregor was the first to finish. "Sirena, you have done it again. The Worbel was superb."

"Thank you, Master Phillary. Thanks to Niccolai for bringing the birds back from the hunt." Her gratitude was well-practiced, as was her quick deflection of praise. She rose from the table seeing that the group was near finished. "I have dessert."

Gregor caught her arm. "Elle and I will take ours in the front room." He stood and swept an arm forward as he looked to Elle, clearly expecting that she'd join him.

"Ma'cadal, Lyall." Elle offered to the Suebhian by way of excusing herself.

"Good sleep, Elle," Lyall responded. It was the literal translation. Elle simply smiled rather than providing the more proper salutation.

"Nicco." She nodded.

His reply was merely a typical low-throated noise. Elle rose from the table and following Gregor's indication, proceeded to the front of the house.

As she entered the sitting room ahead of Gregor, she glanced over the bottles on the liquor table. The wine that would normally have called her name had little appeal. Her immediate, deepest desire was to sip a warming drink, then slip off to bed without more that would require brainpower. What would be the best option for a nightcap?

She spotted the snifters among the glassware and lifted one when Gregor's tenor softly brushed her mind.

'Warm the glass in your hands.' Gregor retrieved a snifter of his own and the bottle with the scripted words: *Phillary Armagnac*, framed by brandywine scrollwork on a fawn-colored background. He took the bottle to the table and sat, holding his glass between strong palms. While Elle's fingers didn't wrap the entire snifter, his near swallowed the stemware.

"What is this liquor?" Elle sat opposite him with the table and chess-like game separating them.

"Armagnac. It is a type of brandy. Also produced from my vineyard." He poured a dose of amber liquid for himself then held the bottle at the ready, waiting for Elle to place her snifter beside his. "I would hold it in your hands a bit before tasting to open up the flavors." He sat back, crossing his legs.

Sirena entered, bearing two tiny fluted dishes with an orange-colored cream. "You're welcome, Master Phillary," she answered the inaudible sentiment, before placing the dessert on the table. She turned to Elle and presented her with a small cloth-wrapped package.

"Yster brought these for you—petals from the Suiren that blooms on the water. Soak them and rest them on your eyes as you turn in for bed. You'll feel like a new woman in the morning!" she said, then made a quick exit.

Disinterested in the sweet, Elle placed the package on the table, retrieved the brandy, and tucked her feet beneath her, curling into the chair. She mirrored how Gregor held the snifter in both palms and slowly smelled the dark, spicy bouquet. With the first small sip, Elle closed her eyes and let it rest on her tongue, absorbing the complexity in the woodsy flavors as it tickled her different taste buds. A larger sip sent warmth into her chest. *'Absolutely delectable.'*

When she opened her eyes, Gregor wore a small, perceptive grin. "When you allow yourself to really feel something is when I hear your thoughts. We will work on that. You'll want to be more careful in what you communicate."

"Wonderful." Elle rolled her eyes. "But it's not like everyone can hear me."

"I don't really know who can and who can't," he said as a matter of fact. "Nicco doesn't seem to hear—at least not always."

Fantastic, Nicco knew too? Elle ran a finger around the rim of the glass, then swirled the liquid, watching the amber revolve. Yster heard before they'd entered the conference, but she had said she didn't hear inside the room when both Cera and Gregor did. "Yeah, it might have something to do with your Flare being Psych too...and maybe with contact. To be honest, I'm not sure how much energy I have to analyze it tonight."

"'Tis nothing to worry over this evening. We have plenty of time."

"I *would* like to hear about this other person Cera mentioned." As Elle finished her Armagnac, he tensed slightly at the mention of Cera.

"The brandy is lovely; may I have another?" Elle placed the snifter on the table beside the bottle, her body loosening under the influence. Knowing that she had nowhere to go but to bed, she accepted the warm detachment the liquor offered. "And what was the deal between you and Cera?"

Gregor swallowed, finishing his own drink, and poured two more. Light from the Clarets was dim against the dark wood, but the flowing tawny liquid found and reflected the glow in the stream that flowed from the bottle's mouth. "Cera isn't important." He cleared his throat and handed Elle her second glass. "I assumed you'd want to hear about the other Flare. I'll be right back."

His heels broke the quiet, traveled past the front door, and halted in his office. Elle remained in the company of the quiet fireplace and glowing flowers. The outside warmth didn't require a crackling fire, but she mused that it would enhance the ambiance of the evening. Her head fell to rest on the back of the chair, exhaustion mingling with a comradery only present in a one-on-one environment with Gregor. Before long, the echo of his boots returned across the hardwood. He handed her a leather-bound book before relaxing back into his own chair.

Opening the book to the title page, with raised brows, she read, "*Terrinian Vasileía*?"

"That is a history of the royalty in Terrináe. You are going to want to read about Vasiliás Renauld..." He passed a long moment absorbed in the bottom of his glass before he added, "And Vasílissa Rema. Although, she was a victim as well as the rest of Terrináe. They were the twentieth Vasiliás and Vasílissa. You'll recall that Edmonde and Edony are the twenty-first."

Elle shifted in her chair to gain a better direct view of her benefactor. Tucking the book into her lap, she asked, "Victim?" She could read the details later.

"As I'm sure you've guessed, Regi Renauld's Flare was Psychological." That was the obvious part, but it was troublesome that Gregor chose his words so carefully. "However, there was an aspect of his Flare that allowed him to reach into others and deliberately place thoughts and pull emotions. He used those to control and coerce people."

"So...I *pulled* emotion from Cera, and I'm now seen as the same threat." Elle pressed her lips together tight, beginning to understand the hesitation in the conference. Her eyes and nose stung, and she swallowed hard. Another sip of the Armagnac thankfully burned away the urge for tears.

Apparently attempting to ease her thoughts, Gregor rushed, "Elle, we did not understand Renauld's Flare or the potential at the time. We don't truly understand yours yet either, but we are committed to helping you to learn. I see that it scares you, too." Gregor remained composed, almost professional as he made these statements, but his eyes were heavy.

"Just...tell me more about the facts. What actually happened with this Renauld character?" Elle sat aside her self-centered sentiment and tried to focus on business and information. Presumably, the more she could learn, the better equipped she'd be to handle what came her way.

'Just have to separate the feeling from the logic, Elle.'

"To begin, he was very charismatic. The whole of the city loved the new Vasiliás." Gregor sat eerily still as he talked, his glass of Armagnac propped on the arm of the chair. He stared in the general direction of the game, but his eyes focused into a distance beyond, seeming to relive a distant past. He finally looked at Elle when he asked, "You do know that they are brother and sister—the Vasileía?"

Once Elle affirmed, he continued, "There is no romance between them, but the unity of twins—female and male—with the Flare is considered sacred. Anyway, they are at liberty to take consorts." His eyes flicked to Elle's, gauging her carefully neutralized reaction. "Without shame, many of the women fell at Renauld's feet, lustful. Some men were enamored as well. He was always gracious in the public eye, demurring at each advance. It was later discovered that he had lured many of these suitors out of the city and done unspeakable things."

Although appalling, such deviance didn't seem so foreign, so Elle didn't reply. There was an ease in academic separation between the horror of factual past events and any emotion at present. Gregor moved back to the alternate timeline, and Elle waited patiently until he shook it off.

After he took another drink, his haunted trance disappeared. "Tendencies strayed far beyond his delinquent sexual itinerary. To further some hidden agenda, he began seeking control over benefactors, advisors, priests, and priestesses." He motioned with his snifter toward the book in Elle's lap. "The details are in the history."

"And the resolution?" she prompted.

He brought in a chest-broadening breath and on the exhale, said, "Execution." In a single swallow, he finished his brandy. "In the aftermath, Terrináe was slow to recover. New benefactors and clerics of several Unities were required to bring society back to a sense of normal. New Vasileía, too." He laughed humorlessly. "It is also how I became Benefactor."

Until the next episode...

Reviews tell an author how much you appreciate their work! Please consider leaving a review on Amazon and Goodreads.

Just a few words and some stars will do.

Character List

Following is a comprehensive list of the characters introduced in The Caeteran Tales to date.

Benefactory Houses

Javine House
Andreas Javine, Benefactor
Yster sur Javine, Entrant
Patrick, First Keeper
Erica, Second Keeper

Arnoldi House
Vittoire Arnoldi, Benefactor

Gustava House
Degna Gustava – Benefactor

Michelli House
Diego Michelli – Benefactor

Smythe House

Phillary House
Gregor Phillary, Benefactor
Niccolai sur Smythe-Phillary
Elle sur Phillary, Entrant
Sirena, Keeper

Sebani House
Bellina Sebani – Benefactor

Sorrell House
John Sorrell – Benefactor

Middlemist House
Camellia Middlemist – Benefactor

Vacant – Benefactor
Hereward "Ward" Smythe – prior Benefactor

Ennead / Holy Unities

First Unity: Ianarius and Iana
Second Unity: Alphinus and Alphiné
Cera d'Alphiné – votara
Devan d'Alphinus – votoro
Third Unity: Liber and Libera
Fourth Unity: Lares and Lara
Fifth Unity: Earys and Anaerys
Sixth Unity: Vaenar and Vaena
Seventh Unity: Niprius and Nipria
Eighth Unity: Ynjeas and Ynja
Ninth Unity: Omneas and Omnia

Cadre Class

Cadre d'Artisans
Lilliana, clothier
Gianna, Lilliana's apprentice

Cadre di Mentori
Natsue, mentor

Entrants in Sixth Induction

Anancathea (aka Nancy)
Blake – chose to return to Earth
Braeden
Elle
Jordan – chose to return to Earth
Quinn

Sonia

Tribes of Tienne h'Ìosal

Suebhi

Ailig, Dion'Mor der Stahm

Mairi, Ailig's daughter

Lothar & Drostan, Mairi's first guard

J'thungi

Sigrün, Dion'Mor der Stahm

N'jari

Unnamed man at the market

Nekhar Suebhi

Unnamed man at the market

Tehruingi

Earth (features in Open Season, 1st of The Caeteran Tales)

Elle Jones

Caleb, Elle's live in boyfriend

Sam, Elle's Cat

Alvita, Elle's assistant

Carmen, Elle's Therapist

Alan D. Schneider, CEO of Traveler's Companies, Inc.

Brenna, Alan Schneider's Receptionist

John Wykoff, CEO of Jewel Systems, Inc.

Kelly Nixon, Elle's boss at Jewel Systems, Inc.

Brian, Elle's lead designer at Jewel Systems, Inc.

Steve Nelson, Recruiter

Glossary

Aithar – /eyth-air/ - Suebhian for father

Ar vaschen d'ehrlichen – formal Suebhian greeting.

Anuri - insect

Bagnio – pleasure house

Bhaumnuts – Treenuts, like almonds

Brüàthr, Brüà – Suebhian for brother

Caetera – /keet-er-uh/ - Name of the new world Elle has been brought to

Caval – /kav-uh-l/ – Horse-like animals – silver-white steeds. Cat-like eyes. Knobby horns. Stout and wide-legged with a full mane covering head and neck, and the same silvery hair forms bells around the hooves. Cavali (pl.)

Cavalback – riding a caval

Cengal – /sing-awl/ - Suebhian meaning the bond between Caval and Rider.

Crith – Suebhian for worm

Cycle – Terrinian measure of time, roughly six months

Decana - A master of a bagnio or an Éhrosi House on the Isles.

Deípno tou Vasíliá – King's Dinner

Dion'Mor der Stahm (m.), Dia'Mor der Stahm (f), Mors der Stahmen (pl) – leader(s) of a Suebhian tribe

Éhros (m.), éhrosa (f), éhrosi (pl) – Courtesans

Entrant - A person selected from Earth to become part of Caeteran Society.

Est – derived from Italian. East.

Gneàrp – Suebhian derogatory term for Terrinians.

Grünpyèr – Green gemstone

Grünen – greens

Grylli - insect

Imèra / Imèri – Day/days

Kav- – A prefix for the caval, used when referring to something relating to the cavali.

Kav-astahr tienne – Caval speed of fire. The caval's gait that is only seen on the plains. Faster, smoother than normal riding. Keeper – Servant and household manager to a benefactory house (usually housekeeper and cook, maybe other duties as well)

Khàinn – Suebhian for dear. As in to a friend. Has the connotation of little.

Khinde – Suebhian for darling, dear. As in a mother or father to a child.

Kurkuma – Suebhian for Turmeric

Ma'cadal – Suebhian for goodnight

Máda / Mádi - Week/weeks

Marchad – Suebhian for a ride (cavalback ride)

Mo – Suebhian for my

Mo Bekänte - honored guest

Monato / monatoj – month / months

Mòran dank – Suebhian for thank you very much

Mentor – A person whose job it is to ease the transition of people into Terrinae.

Noctilucent Claret - Red and purple or white and purple flower, native to the Idris Mountains on Caetera, that is luminescent in the night

Odeum, The – the theater and a great dining hall

Ovest – derived from Italian, West

Pelea shoots – stalks of a plant burned in Unity rituals, namely to prepare non-travelers to cross the rifts.

Pteryx - Bird-like creature raised by the J'thungi

Regi (m.)/ Regina (f.) – Formal address to Terrináe's royalty

Residenze – Neighborhood in Terrináe

Rifter – A servant of the Ninth Holy Unity who has a Physical Flare and can separate rifts between dimensions or planes

Sehr mhath – Suebhian for you're welcome

Stahm, stahmen (pl.) – Suebhian for tribe(s)

Stahmen-mahrk - Tribal market

Sud – derived from Italian, South

Suebhita – Suebhian young girl

Suebhito - Suebhian young boy

Suiren - A flower like the lotus that blooms on a pond.

Terrinian - of Terrináe

Tesoreria - treasury

Tienne h'Ìosal - Flaming Plains

Traveler - A servant of the Ninth Holy Unity, see rifter

Uchi - the name for Natsue's tiny house in Sud Residenze

Unity - Dieties, a pair

Vasileía - Royalty in Terrináe

Vasiliás - King in Terrináe

Vasiliká Palátia - The royal palaces

Vasílissa - Queen in Terrináe

Votoro (m.), Votera (f.), Voteri (pl) - A follower of one of the Unities. For example, Votara d'Iana is a female follower of the First Unity: Iana and Ianarius.

Wapititos - Tiny elk-like creatures native to Caetera and more specifically, the Idris Mountains.

Acknowledgements

Dedicated to my beautiful daughter!

Many, many thanks to all the people who supported me in creating this work. At the top of that list is my family who has given me the space and time to work on this and who provided both a catalyst and inspiration.

My writer's group: Western Suburbs Writers Group in Chanhassen, Minnesota, who provided lots and lots of feedback that went into developing characters, plot, voice, and a number of other writer's skills consistently.

About the Author

My life in Minnesota revolves around my husband, three children, and an incredibly intelligent Bernese Mountain Dog named Delaunay. I've been a Technology Project Manager for more years than I'd like to admit, but stories are my passion. I have always been a voracious reader, lover of worlds, and a "werd nerd." My infatuation with well-developed characters sometimes rivals my relationships with real people. I spend my free time writing, networking with other writers, and occasionally camping "up-north." If you're from Minnesota, you'll get the reference along with "hot dish" and "grey-duck." If you're not from Minnesota, you probably don't want to ask. Note that I'm originally a Texan, and that just never leaves you!

Happy reading and thank you so much!

CPSIA information can be obtained
at www.ICGtesting.com
Printed in the USA
LVHW050923080719
623419LV00006B/541

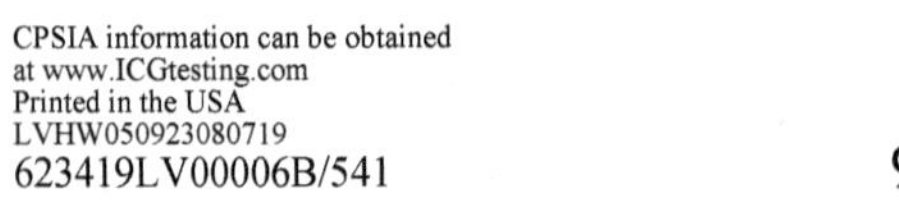